See p. 173 !!
A80 III

31 May, 2018

Also: P. 174 !!!
A80 III

D0838449

MAIGRET AND THE
DEATH OF A HARBOR-MASTER

GEORGES SIMENON

MAIGRET AND THE DEATH OF A HARBOR-MASTER

TRANSLATED FROM THE FRENCH BY
STUART GILBERT

A HARVEST/HBJ BOOK
HARCOURT BRACE JOVANOVICH, PUBLISHERS
SAN DIEGO NEW YORK LONDON

HBJ

COPYRIGHT 1942 BY
HARCOURT BRACE JOVANOVICH, INC.

Library of Congress Cataloging-in-Publication Data
Simenon, Georges, 1903–
Maigret and the death of a harbor-master.
Translation of: Le port des brumes.
"A Helen and Kurt Wolff book."
I. Title
ISBN 0-15-655161-6 (Harvest/HBJ : pbk.)

Printed in the United States of America
First Harvest/HBJ edition 1989
A B C D E F G H I J

MAIGRET AND THE
DEATH OF A HARBOR-MASTER

1. *The Cat in the House*

WHEN the Cherbourg train left Paris, just before three, the cool clear sunlight of an October afternoon still bathed the busy streets. Thirty miles out, when it was nearing Nantes, the lights had been turned on in the compartments. Half an hour later, when the train reached Evreux, it was quite dark. Across the dripping windows nothing could now be seen but a dense fog, through which now and again a railway signal glimmered for a moment, fringed by iridescent sheen.

Slumped in a corner seat, his head resting on the padded back, Maigret watched with half-closed eyes the oddly assorted couple facing him.

Captain Joris was asleep. On that enigmatic, shaven head of his the wig had slipped askew; his clothes were rumpled, travel-stained.

Julie was firmly clutching her bag, a cheap affair in imitation crocodile-skin, and gazing straight in front of her. Tired though she was, she was obviously determined not to give way to fatigue, and to keep up appearances.

Joris. Julie. A puzzling pair.

It was nothing new for Inspector Maigret to have people crashing in like this—out of the blue, so to speak—into his life, and monopolizing it for days, weeks, or even months on end; only to relapse once more into the common herd of nondescripts.

The rumbling wheels set a rhythm to his thoughts, the thoughts that always haunted him at the start of an investigation. Would it be an interesting case or mere routine-work; dull or eventful?

As Maigret gazed at Joris a smile hovered on his lips. An odd bloke! "Bloke" came naturally, for at Headquarters during the last five days this stalwart, stockily built seaman in the early fifties had been known merely as "The Bloke."

Noticing a man behaving in a peculiar manner, dodging in and out amongst the traffic, a constable on duty on the Central Boulevards had taken him into custody. He had been questioned in French. No answer. Seven or eight foreign languages were tried without success. A deaf-mute expert likewise had drawn blank.

A lunatic? He had been searched in Maigret's office. His suit and undergarments were brand-new. Tailor's and shirt-maker's names had been cut out. No identity papers. No wallet. But, tucked into a coat pocket, five crisp thousand-franc notes.

The inquiry had got on everybody's nerves. Police registers and anthropometric records had been ransacked. Telegrams dispatched all over France, and abroad. And from morn till night, under a perpetual cross-fire of questions, "The Bloke" had just gone on smiling, quite happily, to himself. Throughout the ordeal he had not once protested, never shown emotion; sometimes he seemed to make an effort to remember, but gave in almost at once.

Loss of memory? The wig had fallen off his head, and it was found that a bullet had perforated the top of the man's skull, not more than two months previously. The doctors were all admiration; rarely had they seen a damaged skull repaired so neatly.

A new batch of telegrams went out, to hospitals and nursing-homes in France, Belgium, Germany, and Holland. Five strenuous days had been wasted in inquiries on these lines.

Chemical analysis of the stains on the man's clothes and the dust in his pockets had given odd results. Some traces had been found of a fishy substance used as sardine bait and peculiar to the northern coast of Norway, where cod-roes are dried and ground up for this purpose.

Did this mean he came from those parts? Was he a Scandinavian? There were indications that he had made a long railway journey. But how could he have managed it alone, unable to utter a word, and wearing that queer, be-wildered air which made him so conspicuous?

His photograph was published in the papers. A wire came from Ouistreham: *Unknown man identified.* It was followed up by a young woman, who burst into Maigret's office. A young woman with a haggard face, clumsily rouged and powdered; Julie Legrand, "The Bloke's" housekeeper.

So now he was "The Bloke" no longer; he had a name, a place in the community. He was Yves Joris, a retired sea-captain, now harbor-master at Ouistreham.

Julie burst into tears. Julie simply couldn't understand! When she implored him to speak, the man merely gazed at her good-humoredly, as he did at everyone else.

Captain Joris had disappeared from Ouistreham, a small port on the north coast between Trouville and Cherbourg, on September 16. It was now the end of October.

What had he been doing during those six unaccountable weeks?

"He went to the ship-canal," Julie explained, "to take his turn of duty at the lock. High water was late that night. I didn't wait up for him. Next morning, when I went to his bedroom, he wasn't there."

The night had been foggy. He might have missed his

footing and fallen into the lock. It had been dragged without result. Another theory had then been put forward: perhaps he'd had a sudden fancy for a jaunt to Paris, or elsewhere.

"Lisieux. Three minutes' stop."

Maigret stepped out on to the platform to stretch his legs. He filled his pipe again. He had smoked so many pipes since leaving Paris that you could have cut the air in the compartment with a knife.

"Take your seats."

Julie had seized the opportunity to dab her nose with her puff. Her eyes were still red with weeping.

Curious! There were moments when she looked quite attractive, *chic* almost by Parisian standards; others when, though one couldn't say just why, her peasant origin showed definitely through.

She straightened the wig on the Captain's head, casting a glance at Maigret as though to say, "He has only me to look after him, you know." For Joris had no family. For years he had lived alone, except for Julie, whom he called his housekeeper. She always referred to him as "her gentleman."

"He treated me like a daughter."

A quiet man. No enemies; no love-affairs, no vices. After knocking about the world for thirty years, he had settled down for good, it seemed, to blameless domesticity. But he couldn't resign himself to idleness. After giving up the sea he had applied for the post of harbor-master at Ouistreham. He had built a little house there.

Then one fine evening—the sixteenth of September—he'd vanished from the face of the earth; only to reappear in Paris six weeks later, and in what a state!

Julie had been quite shocked at finding him dressed in a

ready-made gray lounge suit. Never before had she seen him in anything but uniform.

She was obviously nervous. Something was weighing on her mind. Every time she turned towards the Captain her look expressed compassion, but something else: an obscure, rankling apprehension. It was he—"her gentleman" —sure enough. And yet, somehow, it wasn't altogether he!

"He'll recover, won't he? Luckily I'm good at nursing."

The moisture on the windows was condensing into turbid drops of water. The Inspector's massive head was gently swaying from side to side with the movement of the train. And all the time, placidly, he was observing the two in front of him: Julie, who had pointed out that they might just as well have traveled Third, as she always did; Joris, who was waking up and gazing dreamily about him.

Another stop, at Caen. The next would be for Ouistreham.

"A village with a thousand or so inhabitants," one of Maigret's colleagues, who came from those parts, had told him. "The harbor's small, but a busy one because of the ship-canal linking the roadstead with the city of Caen. It takes ships of five thousand tons and more."

Maigret made no attempt to imagine what the place was like. He knew too well how misleading such mental pictures always are. He waited, letting his gaze roam constantly towards the wig which hid the pink streak of a scar.

At the time of his disappearance Captain Joris had had thick, dark brown hair, only faintly graying at the temples. Another source of distress for Julie; she couldn't bear the sight of that bald head! And every time the wig slipped awry, she made haste to set it straight.

"Obviously someone was out to kill him," Maigret mused. "That shot was aimed at his head. But obviously, too, someone patched up that head with quite extraordinary skill. He had no money with him when he went; when he was found he had five thousand francs in his pocket."

More was to come. Abruptly Julie opened her bag.

"I forgot to tell you. I brought along his letters."

Nothing much. Ship-chandlers' catalogues. A receipt for a subscription to the Merchant Service League. Picture-postcards from friends still at sea; one from Punta Arenas.

A letter from the Caen branch of the Banque de Normandie. A printed form with the blanks typewritten in:

We beg to advise you that your Account, No. 14173, *has been credited with the sum of* 300,000 *frs.* (*three hundred thousand francs*) *transferred under your instructions from the Dutch Bank, Hamburg.*

Yet Julie had persistently assured him that the Captain wasn't at all well off. Once again Maigret fixed his eyes on the curious pair of people on the opposite seat.

Cod-roe powder. Hamburg. Those obviously "Made-in-Germany" shoes. Bits of a puzzle that only "The Bloke" himself could fit together. And Joris, seeing Maigret's eyes intent on him, promptly responded with the friendliest of smiles.

"Caen. Passengers for Cherbourg, keep your seats. All change for Lion-sur-Mer, Luc, Ouistreham."

Seven o'clock. The air was so saturated with moisture that the platform lamps seemed wrapped in cotton-wool.

"What do we do now?" Maigret asked Julie as they pushed their way through the crowd on the platform.

"There aren't any more trains. In winter the local runs only twice a day."

Luckily there were taxis waiting outside. Maigret was hungry. He decided to take no risks, and dine in the refreshment-room.

Captain Joris was still on his best behavior. He ate whatever was set before him, like a docile, well-mannered child. A railway employee paused for a moment by the table, staring at Joris; then whispered in Maigret's ear:

"Ain't that the harbor-master from Ouistreham, sir?" And tapped his forehead significantly with his forefinger.

When Maigret nodded he moved away, obviously thrilled by the encounter.

When the bill came, Julie's housewifely instincts were properly revolted.

"Just fancy asking twelve francs for a dinner like this! Why, they don't even use butter for their cooking. We'd have done better to go straight home and have our dinner there."

As she spoke, Maigret was thinking: A bullet through his head . . . Three hundred thousand francs. . . . And his keen gaze bored into Joris's mild eyes; his lips set in a hard, menacing line.

The taxi which drew up beside them had been a private car in happier days; now its cushions were battered, it creaked at every joint. The three of them bundled into the back—for the flap-seats had been dismantled—Julie wedged between the two men and crushed by each in turn.

As they approached the house her mind became more and more preoccupied with domestic cares. "I wonder now!" she murmured. "Did I lock the garden gate?"

The fog outside the town was like a solid mass of clotted darkness. They did not catch sight of a horse and cart coming towards them till it was under two yards away. A phantom horse, a phantom cart. And the trees and houses beside the road seemed equally wraithlike.

The driver slowed down to a bare six miles an hour. Even so, a man on a bicycle, emerging suddenly from the fog, blundered into the side of the car. The driver stopped. The cyclist was unhurt.

They crossed the village of Ouistreham. Julie let down the window and called to the driver:

"Drive down to the harbor and cross the swing-bridge. Stop at the house just before the lighthouse."

Outlined by the pale glimmer of a row of gas-lamps, a road ran straight down from the village to the harbor, which was about half a mile away. No one was out at that hour.

"That's the *Sailors' Rest*." Julie pointed through the window at a little café on the roadside. "The lock-keepers spend most of their time there."

After the bridge came a mere apology for a road, floundering through the fenlands bordering the Orne. It led only to the lighthouse and a cottage surrounded by a small garden. Here the car stopped. Maigret observed Joris's movements. He got out of the car of his own accord and walked at once to the gate.

"See that, sir?" Julie exclaimed in a flutter of delight. "He recognized the house. I'm sure he'll be himself again, one day."

She took out her key, opened the creaking iron gate and walked up the gravel path. After paying the driver, Maigret walked quickly after her. Once the car had gone, they were in total darkness.

"Would you strike a light, please? I can't find the key-hole."

A tiny flame. The door opened. A dark form slipped out, brushing against Maigret's calf. Julie entered the hall, turned on the light. Then she halted, gazing at the floor in a puzzled way.

"That was the cat went out just now, wasn't it?"

She took off her hat and coat, hung them on a peg,

walked straight to the kitchen and switched on the light
—unconsciously indicating that this was the room in which
the occupants of the house usually spent their evenings.

A cheerful-looking kitchen. Tiled floor and walls, a big,
well-scoured deal table, gleaming copper pans. Automatically the Captain went up to a wickerwork armchair beside
the fireplace and sat down in it.

"It's queer. I could have sworn I put the cat out, as
usual." She was thinking aloud; her brows were wrinkled.
"Yes, I'm positive. And the doors are locked all right."
She turned to Maigret. "I wonder would you mind, sir,
having a look round the house with me? To tell the truth,
I'm nervous."

So much so that she could hardly bring herself to lead
the way. She entered the dining-room, where the extreme
tidiness, spotless floor and furniture showed that the room
was seldom used.

"Would you mind looking behind the curtains?"

A cottage piano. Some bits of Chinese lacquerware, three
porcelain bowls: souvenirs of the Captain's voyages East.

In the parlor, too, the furniture was equally well kept;
in practically the same state as when it had figured in some
store-window. The Captain followed them, complacent,
almost beaming. They walked up the stairs, which were
carpeted in red. There were three bedrooms, one not in
use.

These rooms, too, were spick-and-span, each object in its
place. And there was a homely fragrance, of country fields
and cooking, in the air.

No one was hiding anywhere. Windows were shut and
bolted. The garden gate was locked, though the key had
been left in it.

"The cat may have got in through a ventilator," Maigret
suggested.

"There isn't one."

They returned to the kitchen. Julie opened a cupboard.

"Would you like something to drink, sir?"

And this was the moment—when she was bustling to and fro, pouring liqueurs into tiny glasses adorned with colored flowers—this was the moment she chose to break down, in a flood of tears.

She shot a furtive, tearful glance at the Captain, who had gone back to his chair. And the sight of him was so distressing that she had to turn away. To give her thoughts a new direction she said to Maigret:

"I'll get the spare-room ready for you."

Her voice was shaken by sobs. She took down a white apron hanging on the wall and dabbed her eyes with it.

"Thank you, I'd rather stay at the hotel. . . . I suppose there is one here?" he added.

She glanced up at a small china clock, of the type that figures as a prize at country fairs, the humble household god of many a French cottage kitchen.

"Yes. It's not too late; you'll find them up. The hotel's just beyond the lock, behind the café I showed you from the taxi."

But she was obviously in half a mind to implore him to stay. She seemed to dread the idea of being left alone with the Captain, at whom she could no longer bring herself to glance.

"Are you sure there's nobody hiding in the house?"

"You could see for yourself there isn't anybody."

"You'll come back first thing tomorrow, won't you?"

She accompanied him to the front door, slamming it behind him the moment he was outside.

The fog was so thick that Maigret could not see where he was treading. Somehow he found his way to the gate. There was the feel of grass underfoot; then of a stony road. As he started down the road he heard a distant sound which, for quite a while, he was unable to account for.

It was like the lowing of a cow, but more mournful, more resonant.

"Of course!" he muttered. "What a fool I am! It's a foghorn."

He had only the vaguest idea of where he was. Then he noticed, vertically below, a patch of water which seemed to be steaming. He was standing on the edge of the lock. From somewhere near at hand there came a sound of turning winches. Where had the taxi crossed the canal? He couldn't remember. Noticing a foot-bridge, he started to cross it.

"Stand back!"

Incredible! The voice was almost in his ear. He had supposed he was quite alone, and all the time there was a man standing within a few feet of him. Peering across the fog, he made out the outlines of a tall black form.

He realized at once why the man had shouted. The foot-bridge on to which he had been about to step began to edge away. It was the lock-gate slowly opening, and the sight was even more impressive when, where the man had been, there towered up, only a yard or so in front, a sheer, black wall, high as a house. Above the moving wall a line of lights glimmered through the fog.

A ship was passing, so close he could have touched it. A hawser dropped beside him; someone snatched it up, dragged it to a bollard, and made it fast.

High up, on the steamer's bridge, a voice cried, "Half speed astern!" then, "Stand by!"

A few moments before, the place had seemed empty, lifeless. Now, as he walked along the edge of the lock, Maigret discovered that the fog was humming with activity. Someone was turning a winch, a man rushed by him with another mooring-rope. A group of customs officers stood waiting for the gangway to be lowered before going on board.

Sightless but skillful movements in a dank mist that fringed the men's mustaches with big drops of water.

"Want to cross?" A voice quite near again. Another lockgate. "Hurry up, or you'll have a quarter of an hour to wait."

As, gripping the handrail, he crossed the bridge, he could hear water gushing in below through the sluices and, remote as ever, the baying of the foghorn. The farther he proceeded, the more the world of fog around seemed teeming with mysterious life. A faint glow of light drew him towards it. He saw a fisherman in a boat moored to the bank, lowering and raising a net slung between two poles. The fisherman cast him a casual glance, then started sorting out the small fry in a basket.

In the zone of brightness made by the steamer's lights he could now see people moving to and fro. They were speaking English on deck. On the edge of the quay a man in a braided cap was checking documents.

The harbor-master, presumably; the man who had taken Joris's place. Like Joris, he was short, but more wiry and alert-looking. He was bandying jokes with the ship's officers.

The visible world had shrunk to a few square yards of relative illumination beyond which lay a netherworld of darkness, hiding land and sea. The sea must be somewhere on his left, where he heard a murmur of waves.

Was it not on just such a night as this that Joris had so mysteriously vanished? Like the fellow yonder, he had been checking ship's papers; cracking jokes, most likely; watching from the corner of an eye the activities of the lock-keepers. Didn't need to see, though. Probably a few familiar sounds told him all he required to know. Just as nobody here looks where he goes, Maigret reflected.

He had just lit a pipe and was frowning at his thoughts. "Compared with these fellows I'm just a damn-fool land-lubber. Everything to do with the sea is right outside my range." And he resented feeling so feebly ineffectual.

The lock-gates opened. The steamer glided into a canal nearly as wide as the Seine at Paris.

"Good evening. You're the harbor-master, aren't you? I'm Inspector Maigret of the Paris police. I've just brought back your predecessor."

"What? Is Joris back? So it was he after all. I only heard of it this morning. Is it a fact that he's . . . ?"

He tapped his forehead.

"Yes—for the moment. Are you stopping here all night?"

"No. We never stay more than five hours at a stretch. Two and a half hours on either side of high water. There are five hours each tide when there's enough water for ships to enter the canal or go out. It's a different time every day. Tonight we've just started, and we'll be at it till three in the morning."

A simple, downright fellow. He spoke to Maigret as to a colleague; as one public servant to another.

"Excuse me." The harbor-master turned and gazed seawards. Nothing was visible, yet he said: "A sailing-boat from Boulogne's made fast to the piles of the jetty, waiting for the gates to open."

"Do you always know in advance what ships are due in?"

"Generally. Steamers especially. Most of them are on a regular run, bringing coal from England and shipping ore from Caen."

"What about a drink?" Maigret suggested.

"Not till the ebb, thanks. I can't get away."

He shouted some orders; the men were quite invisible, but he knew exactly where they were.

"You've been sent here to make an inquiry, eh?"

A sound of footsteps coming up the road from the village. A man walked past the lock-gate; as he walked under a lamp a gun-barrel glinted on his shoulder.

"Who was that?"

"The mayor, off on a duck-shoot. He's rigged up a shooting-pit for himself on the bank of the Orne. His man's there already, I expect, getting things ready for him."

"Think I'll find the hotel open?"

"The *Univers?* Yes. But you'd better get a move on. It's near the time the landlord finishes his game of cards and closes down. And once he's in bed he wouldn't budge for the President himself!"

"Thanks. I'll look you up tomorrow."

"Right. I come on duty here at ten, for the morning tide."

They shook hands; neither had really seen the other's face. A blind man's world—of sightless contacts. There was nothing actually sinister about it, but Maigret was conscious of a certain uncanniness, of something in the air that fretted the nerves; of the sensation of being in a land of shadows, peopled by men who went their secret ways, a life in which he had no place. . . . That sailing-ship, for instance, waiting its turn; it must be quite near, but there wasn't the faintest sign of it.

He passed again the fisherman sitting under his lamp, and was moved to speak to him.

"Any luck?"

The man merely spat into the water. Maigret walked on, furious with himself for making so idiotic a remark.

The last sound he heard before stepping into the hotel was the clatter of the shutters being closed on the top floor of Joris's cottage.

Julie's nervousness. The cat that had slipped out when they were entering the house . . .

"Will the foghorn go on making that blasted noise all night?" Maigret inquired peevishly of the hotel proprietor, who had just approached him.

"As long as the fog lasts. But you get used to it."

He had a restless night—the sort of night that comes of overeating, or when, as a child, one is looking forward to a great treat next day. Twice he rose and pressed his forehead to the icy panes, but all he could see was the empty road and the veering lighthouse-beam struggling to pierce a cloudbank. And all night the foghorn kept on baying, more stridently, it seemed, than ever.

On the second occasion he looked at his watch. It was 4 A.M. There was a clatter of wooden clogs on the road: fishermen tramping down to their boats, baskets slung across their backs.

Almost immediately afterwards, as it seemed to him, there was a banging on his door. It opened before he'd had time to say "Come in." It was the proprietor of the hotel. Seriously upset, judging by his expression.

More time had passed than Maigret had supposed, for sunlight was streaming through the windows. The foghorn, however, was still at it, full blast.

"Get up. The Captain's dying."

"What Captain?"

"Joris. Julie's just rushed down to the village to fetch the doctor. She told me to let you know at once."

Maigret had already pulled on his shirt and trousers. He thrust his feet into his shoes without troubling to lace them up. Nor did he trouble to brush his tousled hair.

He slipped on his coat and ran down the stairs, collarless.

"Won't you have something before you go? A cup of coffee? A glass of rum?"

Maigret shook his head impatiently and rushed out.

Though the sun was bright, the air was nippy. The road was still drenched with dew.

As he hurried across the lock he had a brief glimpse of the sea, a pale expanse of blue; only a narrow strip, for the fogbank began quite near the shore.

On the bridge one of the local police hailed him.

"You the Inspector, sir, from Paris? Good morning, sir. Have you heard—?"

"What?"

"It's horrible, they say. . . . Hullo! That's the doctor's car."

Down in the harbor fishing-smacks were gently rocking at their moorings, dappling the water with glints of red and green. Some sails were set, to dry presumably; each had a number painted on it, in black.

Two or three women were standing outside the Captain's cottage, close by the lighthouse. The door was open. The doctor's car dashed past Maigret and the policeman, who was keeping at his side.

"There's talk of poison. They say his face has gone all green!"

As Maigret entered the house Julie was coming slowly down the stairs. Her eyes were swollen with weeping, her cheeks darkly flushed. The doctor, who was now examining his patient, had bundled her out of the bedroom.

She had had no time to dress, and had slipped an overcoat over her long white nightgown. Her slippered feet were bare.

"It's too terrible, sir. You simply can't imagine . . . Do please go up at once. Perhaps . . ."

When Maigret opened the door, the doctor, who had been bending over the bed, was just straightening up. The expression on his face showed that he had given up hope.

"Police," said Maigret.

"Yes? Quite so. . . . It's all over. Two or three minutes more, perhaps. Strychnine, unless I'm greatly mistaken."

He went to the window and flung it wide open, as the dying man seemed to be gasping for breath. Maigret had a glimpse of the sunlit harbor: fishing-boats and flapping sails, fishermen emptying creels of silvery fish into wooden boxes. And somehow the whole scene looked unreal, like a painted backcloth.

When he turned towards the bed, the dying man's face seemed greener, even more livid than before. Its color was incredible—quite unlike any idea one has of the color of human skin.

The limbs were jerking spasmodically, like the limbs of a grotesque clockwork doll. And yet his look was placid as ever, his features in repose, his eyes fixed on the wall in front of him.

The doctor's fingers rested on his wrist, timing the failing pulse. A moment came when his look conveyed: "Now it's come! He's going. . . ."

But then something extraordinary happened; extraordinary and deeply touching. There had been no knowing if the unfortunate man had got back his reason; certainly there had been no sign of it. Now, of a sudden, his face seemed to come to life. His features quivered like a child's on the brink of tears, in a look of utter, inconsolable distress.

And two big tears welled up, and hovered at the corners of his eyes.

Almost immediately the doctor said in a toneless voice: "He's dead."

Was it possible? The notion of a dead man weeping seemed preposterous. Yet, as a tear that seemed alive trickled off into the hollow of an ear, the man who shed it had ceased to live.

Hearing the sound of footsteps on the stairs, Maigret went out on to the landing and said commandingly:

"No one is to enter the bedroom."

"Is he . . . ?"

"Yes."

He could hear Julie sobbing passionately in the hall and some women trying to console her.

When he went back to the sunlit bedroom, he found the doctor, syringe in hand, administering a heart injection—merely for conscience' sake.

From the window he could see a white cat basking on the garden wall.

2. The Will

SOMEWHERE downstairs, probably in the kitchen, Julie was still giving vent to her distress; Maigret could hear her shrill cries, though the bedroom door was closed.

The window had remained open, and he now saw people pouring helter-skelter out of the village: boys on bicycles, women with babies in their arms, men in clogs. They streamed across the bridge in a small ragged procession, then spread out and hurried towards the Captain's cottage. They were behaving exactly as they would have behaved had a traveling circus been sighted on the road, or had there been a motor accident.

Soon the din outside was such that Maigret shut the window. At once the room took on a different aspect. The garish morning light was mellowed by the muslin curtains to a gentle glow that played discreetly on the polished light-oak chairs, pale pink wall-paper, a bowl of flowers standing on the mantelpiece.

The doctor, Maigret noticed, was holding up to the light the water-bottle and tumbler he had found on the bedside table. He even dipped a finger in the tumbler and touched the tip of his tongue.

"So that was it?"

"Yes. Evidently the Captain had a habit of drinking at night. As far as I can judge, he must have had a drink at about three this morning. What I can't make out is why he didn't call for help."

"For the good reason," said Maigret rather gruffly, "that he was incapable of speaking, or uttering the least sound."

Calling the local policeman, he instructed him to report to the mayor and to the Public Prosecutor at Caen what had happened. There was still a good deal of commotion going on downstairs. Villagers were standing about in groups around the gate; others, to wait in greater comfort, had stretched themselves on the grass along the roadside.

The sand-banks at the harbor entrance were already submerged by the rising tide. A blur of smoke on the horizon showed where a steamer lay at anchor, waiting for high water before entering the lock.

"Have you any idea—?"

The doctor broke off, seeing that Maigret was busy. Between the two windows stood a mahogany writing-desk, and the Inspector had opened it. With the air of frowning concentration he always wore on such occasions he was making a list of the contents of the drawers. At such moments he looked positively churlish. He had lit his fat pipe and was puffing at it slowly, while his thick fingers handled without the least respect the objects they unearthed.

Photographs, for instance. There were dozens of them. Many were the photographs of friends, mostly men in naval uniform and of about the same age as Joris. It was obvious that he had kept in touch with his fellow-cadets of the Brest training-ship, and they wrote to him from every corner of the Seven Seas. Picture-postcards, too; all equally banal whether they hailed from Saigon or from Santiago, with such inscriptions as: "*All the best from Henry,*" "*My third stripe at last!! Cheero! Eugène.*" Most were addressed to "*Captain Joris, S.S. Diana, Anglo-Norman Navigation Co., Caen.*"

Maigret turned to the doctor.

"Had you known the Captain long?"

"Only a few months. Since he became harbor-master. Before that he was on one of the mayor's ships; commanded her for twenty-eight years."

"The mayor's ships?"

"Didn't you know? Our mayor, Monsieur Ernest Grandmaison, is Chairman of the Anglo-Norman. In other words, sole owner of the eleven steamers flying the Company's flag."

Another photograph, this time of Joris himself at the age of twenty-five. Already inclined to squatness, with a broad good-humored face, in which, however, was a hint of obstinacy. A typical Breton.

Finally, in a canvas wallet was a sheaf of documents, ranging from a school award to a master's ticket in the merchant service; some official forms, a birth-certificate, a soldier's service-book, passports.

An envelope fell on the floor. Maigret picked it up. The paper was already yellow with age.

"Is it a Will?" asked the doctor, who had nothing more to do till the investigating magistrate arrived.

Evidently an atmosphere of trust prevailed in Captain Joris's cottage, for the envelope was not even closed. Inside was a sheet of paper, inscribed in a neat, copperplate hand.

I, Yves Antoine Joris, Captain in the Merchant Service, hereby give and bequeath all the real and personal estate of which I shall be possessed at the time of my decease to my servant Julie Legrand, in gratitude for her faithful service.

I instruct her to make the following bequests on my behalf: my dinghy to Captain Delcourt; my china dinner-service to his wife; my carved ivory walking-stick to . . .

Almost all the people whom Maigret had seen working in the fog the night before, the small community of Port

Ouistreham, had been remembered, down to the lock-hand, who was bequeathed a fishing-net—"the trammel hanging in the tool-shed," as the Will described it.

Just then there was a sound of hurried steps behind him. Julie had seized the opportunity, when the women with her were brewing a potion "to cheer the poor dear up," of slipping upstairs. She burst into the room, cast a scared glance around it, then sidled nervously towards the bed. But her courage failed her at the sight of death, and she drew back.

"Is he . . . ?"

She collapsed on to the carpet, murmuring broken phrases. "It can't be true! My poor gentleman! . . . No, I can't believe it."

Gravely Maigret bent down and raised her to her feet. Then, gently mastering her resistance, he shepherded her into the next room, her bedroom. It was in disorder. Clothes scattered on the bed, the basin full of soapy water.

"Who filled the water-bottle on his bedside table?"

"I did. Yesterday morning. At the same time as I put the flowers in the Captain's room."

"Were you alone at the time?"

Julie was still racked by sobs, but her self-possession was returning. Vaguely she sensed the drift of Maigret's questions.

"What are you imagining?" she suddenly demanded.

"I'm imagining nothing! . . . I've just read Joris's will."

"Well, what about it?"

"He leaves everything to you. You're a rich woman."

The only effect of the remark was another flood of tears.

"The Captain was poisoned," Maigret went on. "There was poison in the water on his bedside table."

She swung round on him, her eyes blazing with indignation.

"What are you trying to make out?" she shouted in his face. "Tell me straight! What are you getting at?"

In her excitement she had gripped his arm and was shaking it violently. She looked as if at any moment she might start clawing his cheeks.

"Steady, Julie! Don't lose your head! The inquiry's only just beginning. I'm not hinting at anything. Merely gathering information."

The door was flung open. The village policeman entered.

"The examining magistrate can't be here before the beginning of the afternoon. The mayor was in bed; he'd been out all night duck-shooting. He says he'll come as soon as he can."

The nerves of all were strung to breaking-point. Even the crowd outside, though none of them could have said what they were expecting, were somehow conscious of the tension in the air.

Maigret turned to Julie again.

"Will you be staying here?"

"Why not? I've nowhere else to go."

Maigret asked the doctor to leave the bedroom; then locked the door. He allowed only two women to remain in the house—the lighthouse-keeper's wife and the wife of one of the men working at the lock—to keep Julie company. To the constable he said:

"Don't let anyone in. And see if you can't get the people outside to disperse—without using force, of course."

He walked to the gate, threaded his way through the gaping crowd, and made his way to the bridge. The fog-horn could still be heard, but faintly now, as the wind was blowing off-shore. The tide was still rising.

Two of the lock-hands were already on their way back from the village for their spell of duty. On the bridge Maigret encountered Captain Delcourt, who came up to him at once.

"I say, is it true?"

"That Joris has been poisoned? Yes."

"Who did it?"

The crowd outside the cottage was beginning to break up. The constable's work, evidently, for he could be seen gesticulating, moving from group to group. Maigret wondered what yarn he was telling them. For now their interest had shifted to himself; all eyes were turned in his direction.

"I see the tide's rising. Are you going on duty now?"

"Not yet. The water's still three feet short. See that steamer at anchor in the bay? She's been waiting since six o'clock this morning."

Quite a number of people were hovering in the background, not daring to come nearer: customs officers, the water-bailiff, the head lock-keeper, the skipper of the coast-guard cutter. Farther off, the lock-hands were getting ready for their day's work.

Maigret had now an opportunity of observing in broad daylight the men who had been round him last night, hidden by the fog. The *Sailors' Rest* was only a few steps away. Its windows overlooked the bridge, the lock and jetties, the lighthouse and Joris's cottage.

"How about a drink?" Maigret pointed to the little café. He felt pretty sure that the proposal was in order; that all these people regularly gathered there when the tide was making. The Captain paused to verify the height of the water.

"Right! I've half an hour in hand."

They entered the café, a wooden shack with a bar and

half a dozen tables; after some brief hesitation, the others followed. Maigret beckoned to them to come and join him at his table.

The great thing now was to break the ice, somehow to win their confidence and make them feel at ease with him.

"What's it to be?"

They eyed each other; the constraint had not yet worn off. Then one of them took courage.

"Well, in the morning we usually have a cup of coffee, with a dash of brandy in it."

A woman served the drinks. The people coming from the cottage peeped into the café as they passed; then dispersed about the harbor, reluctant to go home lest they should miss some sensational development.

After filling his pipe, Maigret handed round his pouch. Captain Delcourt preferred a cigarette. The head lock-keeper, however, took a pinch of the tobacco and, blushing a little, put it into his mouth.

"Beggin' your pardon, sir . . ."

"A queer affair, isn't it?" Maigret remarked tentatively.

All had known that some such question was impending; none the less, there followed an embarrassed silence.

"This Captain Joris, now. By all accounts he was a quiet, harmless sort of man. . . ." He paused, covertly observing the men's faces.

"Quiet—that's him!" grinned Delcourt. He was a little older than his late colleague, less careful in his dress, and had, one felt, no aversion from strong liquor. All the same, even while he spoke, he didn't cease watching through the window the progress of the tide, and the steamer, which was now weighing anchor.

"He's moving a bit too soon. If he doesn't watch out, the current from the river will push him on the sand-bank."

"Here's luck! So, I take it, no one here knows what happened on the night of the sixteenth of September?"

"No one. There was a pea-soup fog on, like last night. I wasn't on duty. But I stayed here all the same, having a game of cards with Joris and the other fellows—I mean, the fellows who're here now."

"Did you meet here every night?"

"Practically. There's precious little doing at Ouistreham —in the way of amusement, I mean. . . . Three or four times Joris got one of us to take his hand, when he had to go up to the lock and let a ship through. At nine-thirty he went off duty. He started back in the fog. We all thought he was going home."

"When did you learn he'd disappeared?"

"Next morning. Julie came to ask if we knew anything. She'd gone to bed without waiting up for Joris. Next morning, when she found he wasn't in his room, she was 'struck of a heap,' as she said."

"Had Joris had many drinks?"

"Not he!" put in the customs officer, not wishing to be left out of the conversation. "He never had more than one. And never smoked."

"Oh, by the way . . . Julie and he, were they—well, you see what I mean?"

There was a quick exchange of glances; some men smiled.

"Ask me another! Joris swore there wasn't anything. Only . . ."

The customs officer chipped in again.

"It's not that I'd anything against him, but—well, he wasn't quite the same as the rest of us. Not that he put on airs, only he was a bit stand-offish. He'd never have gone on duty at the lock in clogs, for instance, like Delcourt here does now and again. He'd join us in a game of cards

most evenings, but he'd never drop in for a drink in the
daytime. He didn't call the fellows at the lock by their
Christian names. . . . I wonder if you see what I'm driving at?"

Maigret saw it very well. He had spent some hours in
Joris's home, the tidy, well-appointed home of a man of
modest means and quiet tastes. The men here were of a
very different type—rougher, more free-and-easy in their
ways. Here short drinks went down, he guessed, at a high
speed; voices rose, the atmosphere grew thick, the talk a
trifle bawdy on occasion.

Joris dropped in simply for a game of cards, never talked
about his private affairs, and departed after a single drink.

"They've been together for eight years and more. She
was sixteen when she came to him—and a slovenly, badly
dressed little thing she was in those days."

"And now?"

Without being called, the waitress came up with a bottle
of brandy and poured another tot into the glasses, where
there now remained only some dregs of coffee. This, too,
was doubtless a ritual of the place.

"And now she's—well, you've seen our Mademoiselle
Julie. She fancies herself. At our local hops, for instance,
she won't dance with anybody and everybody, not she!
And if they treat her like a servant when she's shopping,
she flies off the handle. That's how she is. You'd never believe her brother—"

The lock-keeper gave the customs officer a warning look,
which Maigret intercepted.

"Ah, she has a brother," he remarked.

"The Inspector's bound to hear of it sooner or later," the
man remarked. Clearly the "laced" coffee he was drinking
was not his first of the day by any means. "Her brother did
eight years' hard. Got soused one night at Honfleur. There

was a whole crowd of 'em painting the town red. The police tried to stop it and he laid a policeman out. The poor chap died next month."

"A sailor, is he?"

"He served on deep-sea craft before he came back to these parts. Now he's on a coasting-schooner, the *Saint Michel* of Paimpol."

Captain Delcourt, who had been showing signs of impatience, rose to his feet.

"Come along! Time to be off."

"What's the hurry? Steamer's not in the lock yet," grumbled the customs officer, who seemed disinclined to move.

Only two of the group remained. Maigret beckoned to the waitress, who came back with the bottle.

"Does the *Saint Michel* often call here?"

"Now and then."

"Was she here on the sixteenth of September?"

The customs officer hesitated, then, turning to the man beside him, said:

"Well, he could have found it out from the lock register anyhow, couldn't he? . . . Yes, she was here. As a matter of fact, they had to stay in the outer harbor all night because of the fog, and didn't sail till daybreak."

"Know where they sailed for?"

"Southampton. I checked their papers. They'd loaded millstone grit at Caen."

"And Julie's brother hasn't been seen in this part of the world since then, I take it?"

This time the customs officer drew a deep breath, pondered, and drained his glass before replying.

"Better ask that of the folk who say they saw him around yesterday. Can't say I saw him, myself."

"Yesterday?"

The man made an evasive gesture. A steamer was gliding past between the stone walls of the lock, its black bulk towering above the countryside, its funnel higher than the trees fringing the canal.

"Must be going."

"So must I."

Maigret beckoned to the waitress.

"How much?"

"Oh, you're sure to be coming here again. I'll chalk it up."

When Maigret left the café there were still some people hanging about, waiting for something to happen, outside the Captain's cottage. When they caught sight of the Inspector they pretended to be gazing at the English ship passing through the lock. Just then a man came striding down from the village. The Inspector judged him to be the mayor, of whom he had had a glimpse the night before.

A man between forty-five and fifty, very tall, pink-cheeked, inclined to stoutness. He wore gray shooting-kit and gaiters. Maigret went towards him.

"Monsieur Grandmaison? I am Inspector Maigret of the *Police Judiciaire*."

"Pleased to meet you." The tone was noticeably off-hand.

The mayor stared at the café, then at Maigret, then back at the café. It was easy to guess what he was thinking. "Queer that a big man in the Paris police should keep such low company!"

They continued walking towards the lock, which lay between them and the cottage.

"I hear Joris is dead."

"That's so," said Maigret curtly. He did not much like the mayor's attitude.

Yet it was quite in keeping. The attitude of the bigwig

of a small country town who deems himself the center of the universe, affects the dress of a country squire, and pays tribute to democracy by shaking hands with all and sundry, greeting the country folk with casual *bonhomie* and, on occasion, patting their children on the head.

"Think you'll catch the murderer? After all, it was you who brought Joris back, and— Excuse me."

He went up to the water-bailiff, who evidently acted as his gillie on his shooting expeditions, for he said:

"All the wattles on the right of the pit need straightening. And one of the decoys is no use whatever; this morning he seemed more dead than alive."

"Very good, sir."

Before rejoining Maigret the mayor took the opportunity of shaking hands with the harbor-master.

"Good morning, Captain."

"Good morning, Mayor."

"What were we talking about? Oh, yes. . . . Is there any truth in all this talk about a wound in Joris's head that had been sewn up, and his having gone mad, and all the rest of it?"

"Was Captain Joris a friend of yours?"

"Joris was in my employ for twenty-eight years. I thought highly of him. He was conscientious in his work."

"Honest?"

"Almost all my men are honest."

"What was his pay?"

"Well, it varied—on account of the war, you know, which upset shipping conditions. Still, he made enough to buy that cottage of his. And I should say he'd twenty thousand francs or so put away in the bank."

"No more?"

"I doubt it. Say five thousand more, at most."

The upper lock-gate was opening, and the steamer about

to move into the canal. Another ship, coming from Caen, was waiting to take its place and put out to sea.

It was a calm, fine morning. People on the road followed the two men with their eyes. From the deck of the steamer, English sailors glanced down now and then at the crowd, as they went about their duties.

"What's your idea, Mayor, of Julie Legrand?"

"A little fool. Joris treated her far too well and she's had her head turned. She fancies herself—how shall I put it?—she fancies herself above her station."

"And her brother?"

"Never met the man. But by all accounts he's a black-guard."

They were near Joris's gate. Children were still hanging round it, playing—waiting for something exciting to happen.

"What was the cause of his death?"

"Strychnine poisoning."

Maigret was wearing his surliest look, walking slowly, his hands thrust deep in his overcoat pockets, his pipe between his teeth. The pipe seemed made to match his massive face; it took the best part of a quarter of an ounce of tobacco.

The white cat was still lying on the wall, basking in the sun. It took to its heels as the two men came up.

"Aren't you coming in?" The mayor was surprised to see Maigret halt at the gate for no apparent reason.

"Just a moment. Do you think Julie was the Captain's mistress?"

"How the devil should I know?" There was a note of peevishness in Monsieur Grandmaison's voice.

"Did you visit his house often?"

"Never set foot in it. Joris had been one of my employees. And that being so . . ." A would-be aristocratic smile filled out the pause.

"If you don't mind," the mayor continued, "we'll get it over as quickly as possible. I have people coming for lunch."

"Are you married?"

His hand still on the gate-latch, an obstinate look on his face, Maigret stuck to the idea that was running in his head.

Monsieur Grandmaison drew himself up to his full height, all but six feet, and glared down at him. The Inspector noted that, though the mayor did not actually squint, there was a slight asymmetry in his eyes.

"Let me tell you, Inspector, if you continue speaking to me in that tone you'll have reason to regret it. . . . Now then, show me whatever you have to show."

He opened the gate himself and walked up to the door. The constable on duty on the threshold stood back deferentially.

The kitchen door had glass panels. Something struck Maigret at once: the two women were there all right—but where was Julie?

"She's gone up to her room, sir, and shut herself in. We couldn't get her to come down again."

"Any special reason for her going up like that?"

The lighthouse-keeper's wife explained.

"She was feeling better. Still crying a bit, but not so hard, and starting to chat with us. 'Have something to eat, Julie,' says I, and off she goes to the cupboard. . . ."

"Yes? And then?"

"I couldn't make it out. She seemed all in a flutter, and rushed out like a mad thing. Then we heard her slam her door and turn the key."

The cupboard contained only kitchen utensils, a basket

of apples, some soused herrings on a dish, and two dirty
plates, the streaks of grease on which suggested there had
been cold meat on them.

"May I venture to suggest, Inspector," said the mayor
with labored politeness, "that we make a start? It's half-
past eleven. I hardly think that the doings of that young
woman . . ."

Maigret locked the cupboard, pocketed the key, and
strode heavily towards the staircase.

3. *The Store-Cupboard*

"OPEN the door, Julie."

No answer. Only the sound of a body slumping on to the bed.

"Open the door."

Silence. Maigret lunged against the door with his shoulder. The screws holding the lock gave way.

"Why wouldn't you let me in?"

She was not crying. She made no movement. Huddled up on the bed, she was staring straight in front of her, steady-eyed. Only when the Inspector was dangerously near did she make a move. Jumping off the bed, she ran towards the door.

"Leave me alone!" she panted.

"Then—give me the letter, Julie."

"What letter?"

She took a combative tone, hoping to brazen out her lie.

"Did the Captain allow your brother to come and see you here?"

No answer.

"I see. He forbade it. But your brother came all the same. In fact, he paid you a visit, I understand, the night that Joris disappeared."

A hard, almost murderous glance.

"The *Saint Michel*," Maigret continued calmly, "was in harbor. Quite natural he should look you up. Just one question, by the way. When he comes, you give him something to eat, don't you?"

"You beast!" she muttered under her breath.

"He came here while you were in Paris. As you were away, he left a note for you. To make sure that you and no one else would find it, he put it in the store-cupboard. Give me the note."

"I've thrown it away."

Maigret glanced at the empty grate, the closed window.

"Hand it over, Julie."

She stiffened up, not like a woman at bay, but like a child in a temper. So much so that the Inspector couldn't help murmuring in an almost elder brotherly tone:

"You silly kid!"

The note had merely been slipped under the pillow of the bed where she was lying. But even now she would not give in. She flung herself on the Inspector, tried to wrest the letter from his hand. Her childish rage amused him.

Prisoning her wrists, he said gruffly, "That's enough of that," and proceeded to read the ill-written, misspelt missive.

If you come back with your genleman look after him well as theres some bad lots got a down on him. Ile be back in 2 or 3 days with the ship. Dont look for the cutletts as Ive eten them. Yr loving brother.

Maigret stared at the floor, so puzzled that he seemed to have forgotten Julie's presence. . . .

A quarter of an hour later he was in the harbor-master's office. Delcourt informed him that the *Saint Michel* was reported in at Fécamp and, if the nor'wester held, should reach Ouistreham next evening.

"So you know the exact position of all the ships in these waters?" Maigret's eyes roved thoughtfully the shimmering expanse of sea, from which rose far out a single plume of smoke.

"Yes, we're in touch all along the coast. Look! That's the list of ships due in today." He pointed to a blackboard on the wall, with names chalked on it. "Had any luck in your inquiry? By the way, take everything folks tell you with a grain of salt. Even quite worthy folks. You'd never believe the amount of backbiting that goes on in this place." Delcourt waved to the skipper of a cargo-boat that was moving across the harbor, gazed at the *Sailors' Rest*, and sighed. "That's how they are, worse luck!"

At three o'clock the Prosecutor and his colleagues had finished their inspection and, under the thrilled gaze of the little knot of people outside Joris's gate, filed out to the four cars awaiting them on the road.

"Lots of duck round here, I suppose?" a high official remarked to Monsieur Grandmaison, after a glance across the fens.

"It's been a poor season. But last year . . ."

Monsieur Grandmaison broke off and hurried to the leading car, which was just beginning to move.

"You'll drop in at my place for a moment, I hope. My wife's expecting you."

Maigret had kept in the background. Now, with the bare minimum of affability, the mayor addressed him.

"Step in, Inspector. We hope you'll join us—needless to say."

Only Julie and the two women were left in the cottage. The constable stood at the doorway, on watch for the motor hearse that was coming to take the body to Caen.

In the four cars a mood of cheerfulness prevailed—like that on the way back from a funeral when the mourners are boon companions and glad to have got it over. The mayor chatted to the Deputy Prosecutor, while Maigret sat uncomfortably on the flap-seat.

"If I had my own way, I'd live here all the year round.

Unfortunately my wife doesn't care much for the country. The result is, we're mostly at our house in Caen. . . . My wife's just back from Juan-les-Pins, where she's been staying with the children."

"How old is he now, your son?"

"Fifteen."

The lock-keepers watched the car go past. Soon the mayor's country house came into view, an enlarged edition of a Norman cottage, its grounds surrounded by white palings and studded with terra-cotta animals.

Madame Grandmaison, in a dark silk dress, welcomed each guest with a discreetly modulated smile—quite the accomplished hostess. The drawing-room door stood open. On a table in the smoking-room stood an array of liqueurs, boxes of cigars.

All these people, Maigret noticed, knew each other well. They evidently belonged to the same set at Caen. A white aproned maid took the men's coats and hats.

"So you'd never been to Ouistreham before, Judge, though you've been living all these years in Caen?"

"Twelve years, madame, to be precise. . . . Ah, there's Mademoiselle Gisèle."

A girl of fourteen, but older than her years in bearing—she had all her mother's poise—had come in, and was shaking hands with the guests. . . . Meanwhile no one had thought fit to introduce Maigret to the lady of the house.

"I expect that after what you've just been looking at you'd prefer something stronger than a cup of tea. Yes? A glass of liqueur brandy. . . . Is your wife still at Fontainebleau?"

People were talking on all sides of him. Maigret heard snatches of their conversation.

"No, ten duck in a night is a very good bag indeed. . . .

One doesn't feel the cold, I assure you. Anyhow, I keep a fire going in my shooting-pit."

Another voice: "I suppose the shipping slump has hit people rather hard."

"Well, that depends. Here we hardly notice it; none of our vessels are laid up. Of course small shipowners, especially those with only coasting-schooners, are beginning to feel the pinch. In fact, most of the people who own schooners are trying to get rid of them; they don't cover expenses."

"No, madame"—it was the Deputy Prosecutor speaking, just beside Maigret. "There's no reason to feel alarmed. The mystery, if there is a mystery, about the man's death will soon be cleared up. Isn't that so, Inspector? What? Haven't you been introduced? Allow me. . . . This is Inspector Maigret, one of the leading lights of our *Police Judiciaire*."

Maigret was at his most unbending, his expression as little amiable as might be. He cast a curious glance at his hostess's young daughter as she proffered him smilingly a plate of fancy cakes.

"No, thanks."

"Really? Don't you like sweet things?"

A voice said: "Here's luck!"

"Here's the best to our charming hostess!"

The Public Prosecutor, a tall, lean man in the early fifties, who in spite of thick-lensed glasses saw with extreme difficulty, drew Maigret aside.

"Needless to say, I give you a free hand. Only please ring me up daily to keep me posted. What's your theory of the crime? A woman at the bottom of it, eh?" Just then Monsieur Grandmaison approached, and he went on in a louder tone: "Anyhow, you're in luck having a mayor to deal with like our friend here. He'll do all he can to help you. . . . Isn't that so, Grandmaison? I was just telling the Inspector . . ."

"If he likes to stay with me, we'll be very glad to have him here. . . . I suppose you're putting up at the hotel, Inspector?"

"Yes. Thanks for your invitation, but the hotel's much handier for the harbor."

"Do you really think you'll pick up any useful information at that pub? Let me put you on your guard, Inspector. You don't know Ouistreham. Those fellows who spend all their time soaking at the pub are apt to let their imaginations run away with them. For the sake of a good yarn they'd accuse their fathers and mothers of any crime!"

"Suppose we talk of something else?" Madame Grandmaison put in with an amiable smile. "Do have a cake, Inspector. No? You haven't a sweet tooth?"

Twice running! Damn these women! By way of protest, Maigret all but fished his huge pipe out of his pocket.

"I'm afraid I must be off. Must get on with my inquiry," he said rather ponderously.

They made no effort to detain him; it was obvious that they no more desired his presence than he desired to stay.

Once outside, he filled his pipe and walked slowly down to the harbor. He was already a familiar figure. Everyone knew that he had stood a round of drinks at the café, and hailed him with a certain friendliness.

From the quayside he saw the car conveying Joris's body to Caen receding in the distance, and had a glimpse of Julie at one of the ground-floor windows; the other women were trying to coax her back into the kitchen.

A group had gathered round a fishing-smack that had just come in, and were watching the crew sort out their catch. The customs officers were lounging on the bridge, whiling away the time till the next ship came in. The harbor-master accosted Maigret.

"I've just had confirmation of the news about the *Saint Michel;* she'll be in tomorrow. She's been three days in dock at Fécamp, it seems, having her bowsprit repaired."

"Tell me, does she ever have dried cod-roe amongst her cargo?"

"Cod-roe? No. It's shipped from Norway in small freighters or Norwegian steamers. But Caen isn't one of their ports of call. They go straight to the sardine ports, Concarneau, Sables d'Olonne, Saint-Jean-de-Luz, and so on."

"And seal-oil?"

The captain looked much surprised.

"On the *Saint Michel?* Why on earth—?"

"Just an idea."

"No. These coasters almost always carry the same cargoes: vegetables, especially onions, for England, coal for the Breton ports, stone, cement, slates, and that sort of thing. . . . By the way, I've been asking the men at the lock about the *Saint Michel's* last call. She came in from Caen at the tail of the tide. The staff were going off duty. Joris pointed out that the water was too low; it wouldn't be safe to put out to sea in thick weather like that. But the skipper insisted on being let through the lock, so as to be ready to sail the first thing in the morning. They spent the night moored in the outer port. At low tide they took the ground and they didn't move till about nine."

"Was Julie's brother on board?"

"Must have been. There's only three of them: the skipper, who owns the boat, and his two men. Big Louis . . ."

"The ex-convict?"

"Yes. He's called 'Big Louis' as he's a great hefty fellow; he could strangle you with one hand!"

"A tough customer, eh?"

"If you asked the mayor or any of the local bigwigs they'd say yes. Personally, I never met the man before he went to jail. And he isn't often here. All I know is that he's never given us any trouble at Ouistreham. He drinks, of course. But you can never tell with him. Always sort of half-seas-over, if you see what I mean. He just mooches about the harbor—I suppose it's that queer lopsided walk of his that puts some folk off. An odd customer! Still, the skipper of the *Saint Michel* swears by him."

"He came here while his sister was in Paris, didn't he?"

No answer. Delcourt merely looked blank. And Maigret realized at that moment that he'd never get at the whole story; the sea-going folk hung together, weren't going to give one another away.

"After all, he's not the only one."

"What do you mean by that?"

"Nothing much. . . . Only I heard talk of a stranger who'd been prowling about. Just gossip."

"Who saw him?"

"Afraid I don't remember. You know the way folk talk. . . . What about a drink?"

For the second time Maigret entered the café; this time hands were stretched towards him.

"Those blokes from Caen made a quick job of it, I hear."

"What's yours?"

"A glass of beer, thanks."

There had been bright sunshine all day. Now the light was paling; strands of mist were creeping lazily between the trees, steam rising from the canal.

"Looks like another thick night," the captain sighed.

Just then there came a distant hooting.

"That's the light buoy at the entrance of the fairway."

Maigret asked point-blank:

"Did Captain Joris often go to Norway?"

"Yes, when he was in the Anglo-Norman. Especially just after the war, when we were so short of wood. Nasty cargo, timber; leaves no room to work a ship."

"Did you work for the same company?"

"Only for a while. I mostly served with Worms & Co., of Bordeaux. 'On the ding-dong' as we used to call it— always the same run, Bordeaux to Nantes and back again. Eighteen years of it I had!"

"Any idea who Julie's parents were?"

"Fisher-folk. She was born at Port-en-Bessin. Fisher-folk in a manner of speaking—her father never did a stroke of work if he could help it. He died in the war. I expect her mother's still selling fish in the street, when she isn't putting down red wine in the pubs."

For the second time, thinking of Julie, Maigret smiled to himself. He remembered her appearance in his Paris office, in a neat blue tailor-made costume, quite the prim young lady. Then the scene that very morning when she had struggled with him, like a child in a tantrum, to prevent him reading her brother's letter.

Joris's cottage was already almost blotted out by the rising mist. There was no light in the bedroom from which the corpse had been removed, or in the dining-room. Only the hall-lamp could be seen, though doubtless the lights were on in the kitchen, where the two neighbors were keeping Julie company.

Some lock-hands entered the café; discreetly they selected a table at the far end for their game of dominoes. The lighthouse lit up.

"The same again." The captain pointed to the empty glasses. "My shout."

In a curiously muffled voice Maigret inquired:

"If Joris were alive, where would he be at this precise moment? Here?"

"No. At home. In slippers, in front of the fire."

"In which room, do you think?"

"In the kitchen. Reading his paper. After that, he'd settle down to a book on gardening—his latest fad. He was crazy about flowers. You've only got to look at his garden —full of 'em, though it's late in the year for flowers."

The others grinned, secretly a little ashamed of themselves for not being "crazy about flowers" and preferring to spend their leisure in a pub.

"He never went shooting?"

"Very seldom. Only when someone asked him to join in a shoot."

"The mayor, for instance?"

"Yes; when the duck were in, they sometimes went together to the mayor's shooting-pit in the fens."

The café was badly lighted and it was difficult to see the domino-players across the haze of smoke. A big stove made the atmosphere still more oppressive. Outside was twilight —a wintry dusk to which the fog added a special, rather eerie gloom. The foghorn was still baying. Maigret's pipe sizzled.

Leaning back in his chair, he half closed his eyes, trying to piece together the scraps of information he had amassed so far. "Joris disappeared for six weeks, then came back with his skull split and sewn up." He was unaware that he had said it aloud. "And no sooner was he home than he was poisoned.

"It was only the next day that Julie found the note left in the cupboard by her brother." Maigret heaved a deep sigh before summing up.

"It comes to this. There was an attempt to kill him. Then he was carefully patched up again. Then he was killed outright. Unless . . ." For the three facts didn't hang together. And a possible explanation had suggested itself, possible but so grotesque that it took his breath away. "Suppose, the first time, it wasn't an attempt to kill him; only to deprive him of his reason?"

Hadn't the Paris doctors said that the operation must have been performed by an extremely skillful surgeon? But, to deprive a man of his reason, would one have to split his skull? And, in any case, what proof was there that Joris's mind was permanently affected?

Keeping respectful silence, the others were gazing at the Inspector. Without speaking, the customs officer signaled to the waitress: "Another round of drinks, please."

In the stuffy room everyone was darkly brooding, lost in thoughts that drink had slightly fuddled.

Three cars passed on the road outside: the officials from Caen returning from the Grandmaisons' reception. . . . By this time Captain Joris's body was lying in cold storage at the Medico-Legal Institute.

There was no sound but the click of dominoes on the deal table at the far end of the room. Gradually, it seemed, the mystery of Joris's death was being brought home to the minds of all present. It weighed on them like something almost palpable that had materialized from the smoke-bound air. Faces grew glum; the junior customs officer was so perturbed that he rose, saying nervously:

"I'd better be going. My wife's expecting me."

Maigret handed his tobacco-pouch to the man next him, who passed it on. Then a voice was heard, Delcourt's.

He too was getting up; he had had enough of the atmosphere of gloom that had settled on the room.

"How much, Marthe?"

"Two rounds? Nine francs seventy-five. And three ten from yesterday."

There was a general move. As the men filed out, damp air poured in by the open door.

Each went homewards in his own direction. Across the baying of the foghorn footsteps rang, receding.

For a while Maigret stood listening to the footfalls scattering in all directions: heavy steps, sometimes slowing down abruptly, sometimes flurried. And he realized that, though one couldn't say how it had come about, fear had taken hold of them.

All those men making for their homes were frightened of something, some vague peril threatening each and all, some unforeseeable disaster; afraid of the dark, afraid of the lights. . . . Thinking, perhaps: "Whose turn next?"

Maigret knocked out his pipe and buttoned up his overcoat.

4. *The Schooner*

"THAT all right, sir?" the hotel-keeper inquired anxiously as each course was served.

"Quite all right." As a matter of fact, Maigret hardly knew what he was eating.

He had the big hotel dining-room—made to hold forty or fifty guests—to himself. It was a hotel for summer visitors, furnished like all seaside hotels, flowers in vases on every table.

This, the holiday-makers' Ouistreham, had no truck with the Ouistreham that interested the Inspector and which, to his great satisfaction, he was beginning to understand. What he always disliked in an inquiry was its start, the first contacts, the preliminary fumblings and false impressions.

This town of Ouistreham, for instance. In Paris he had pictured it, quite wrongly, as a seaport in the style of St. Malo. Then, on the night of his arrival, he had judged it a thoroughly depressing place, inhabited by surly, uncommunicative people.

Now he was on easy terms with it, felt positively at home here. Ouistreham was just an ordinary village at the end of a short road lined by stunted trees. The only part of it that mattered was the harbor: a lock, a lighthouse, Joris's cottage, the *Sailors' Rest*.

And, also, what might be called the "rhythm" of the port—two tides every twenty-four hours, which timed the movements of the little group of men concerned with the canal-lock, and of the fishermen he had watched passing with their baskets.

Certain words, too, had acquired for him a clearer meaning: harbor-master, coaster, cargo-boat. Using eyes and ears to good effect, he had learnt the rules of the game.

Still, the problem which had brought him here hadn't been solved. Indeed, he was as far from a solution as ever. However, he had done the preliminary spadework; got a hang of the people involved, their mode of living, their daily routine. So far, so good. . . .

"Will you be staying long?" The hotel-keeper had himself brought Maigret's coffee.

"Can't say."

"Lucky this didn't happen in the season. It would have done us no end of harm."

Maigret knew by now that there were four distinct Ouistrehams: Port Ouistreham, the village of Ouistreham, residential Ouistreham (with a few private houses like the mayor's along the main road), and lastly Ouistreham-on-Sea, at present out of action.

"Are you going out, sir?"

"Yes. I'll have a stroll before turning in."

The tide was near the full. The weather had turned much colder, and the fog, dense as ever, was forming into drops of icy water.

Everything was in darkness. All the houses were closed and shuttered. Nothing could be seen but the glow of the lighthouse, blurred like a tear-dimmed eye. But from the lock came sounds of people talking.

A short blast of a steamer's whistle. A green light and a red showed up; a dark bulk loomed above the lock wall. Maigret knew enough by now to guess what was happening down there. A steamer was coming in. A shadowy form was picking up the mooring-rope, making it fast to the nearest bollard. Presently, from the bridge, the captain would shout an order to go astern, to take his way off.

Delcourt came up; he gazed anxiously towards the jetty. "What is it?"

"Can't make out." He screwed up his eyes as if by an effort of will he could make them pierce the inky darkness of the foreshore. Two men were beginning to close the lock-gates. He shouted to them: "Hold on a minute!" Then suddenly exclaimed: "Yes, it's he!"

At the same moment, less than fifty yards away, someone bawled:

"Ahoy, Louis! Down jib and stand by to come alongside, port side to."

The voice came from below, from the pool of darkness where the jetties lay. A speck of light approached. Then came sounds of someone walking on a deck, of canvas falling with a rattle of rings along the forestay.

A mainsail glided by, so close they could have touched it.

"How the devil did they manage it?" Delcourt exclaimed in a puzzled tone. Then, turning towards the schooner, he shouted:

"Carry on! Shove her nose in under the port quarter of the steamer or you'll foul the gates."

A man with a hawser had sprung ashore, and now, his arms akimbo, was gazing round him.

"Is that the *Saint Michel?*" Maigret asked.

"Yes. She must have traveled like a racing-yacht."

A hurricane-lamp on the deck beneath cast a wavering light on a pile of ropes, a cask, the form of a man who suddenly let go the tiller and ran to the schooner's bows.

The lock-hands came up one by one and fell to gazing at the schooner with unwonted interest.

"Get back to the gates, boys!" Delcourt called to them. "Man the winches!"

Once the lock-gates closed, water poured in through the sluices and the schooner began to rise. The gleam of light drew nearer. Soon the deck of the *Saint Michel* was almost level with the quay. The man on board hailed Delcourt.

"Evening, captain!"

"Good evening." Delcourt sounded ill at ease. "You made a record run."

"Aye; we had the wind behind us, and Louis set every stitch of sail. We overhauled a steamer on the way."

"Going to Caen?"

"Aye, I unload there. What's the news, this end?"

He was two yards from Maigret, "Big Louis" only a trifle farther off. But they could barely see each other. Only the skipper and the harbor-master did the talking. Delcourt, puzzled what to answer, turned to Maigret.

"Is it true that Joris has come back?" the skipper asked. "There was something in the papers about it, I heard."

"He came back and he's gone again."

"Eh? What's that?"

Louis had moved a step nearer, his hands in his pockets, one shoulder higher than the other. In the darkness he gave the impression of a big, rather loosely built fellow, with nothing distinctive except his slouch.

"He's dead."

Louis had come so close to Delcourt that he could have touched him.

"What's that? Dead?" he growled.

It was the first time Maigret had heard his voice. A husky, drawling voice; an intonation slovenly as the man's way of holding himself. It was still impossible to make out his face.

"He was poisoned the night he got back." And meaningly, Delcourt made haste to add: "This gentleman is the Inspector of Police who's holding the inquiry."

A load off his mind. For some minutes he had been wondering how to break the news. Was he afraid the crew of the *Saint Michel* might give themselves away?

"Ah, you're in the police, sir?" the skipper muttered.

The schooner was still rising. The skipper swung himself over the bulwarks on to the quay, but hesitated before holding out his hand to Maigret.

"An odd affair!" he exclaimed, his mind still on Joris.

He too seemed ill at ease; even more so than Delcourt. Louis's tall form swayed in the darkness, his head cocked on one side. He grunted some words that Maigret failed to catch.

"What did he say?"

"He said in *patois:* 'Dirty work!' "

"What was dirty work?" Maigret asked the ex-convict. But the man merely stared at him. They were near enough now to see each other's faces. Louis's was puffy and one cheek seemed larger than the other—or perhaps it was his trick of keeping his head on one side that made it seem so. Big shallow eyes, coarse features. An unprepossessing face.

"You were here yesterday," the Inspector said to him.

The water in the lock had found its level and the upper gates were opening. The steamer was already entering the canal, and Delcourt had to run to ascertain her tonnage and last port. Someone shouted from the bridge: "Nine hundred tons. Rouen."

The *Saint Michel,* however, stayed in the lock. The men standing by to handle her seemed conscious of something unusual in the air and waited, each at his post, pricking up his ears.

Delcourt was jotting down in his notebook the information given as he walked back.

"Well?" asked Maigret impatiently.

"Well—what?" Louis rumbled. "You said I was here yesterday. I was."

It was hard to follow what the man said; he had a way of speaking with his lips closed, and mumbling as if his mouth were full. Added to this, a broad North-Breton accent.

"Why did you come here?"

"To see my sister."

"And since she was away you left a note for her."

Meanwhile, from a corner of his eye, Maigret was taking stock of the owner of the schooner. He was dressed exactly like his men and looked more like a rather superior boatswain than the skipper of a coaster.

"We stopped three days at Fécamp," he now put in. "So Louis took the opportunity of going to see the girl."

The men posted round the lock were keeping quite still, all eagerness not to miss a word. The foghorn was still blaring. The fog had thickened into a drizzle and the cobbles underfoot gleamed darkly.

A hatchway opened in the schooner's deck, a head peeped out. Tousled hair, a bushy beard.

"What's up? Why ain't we moving?"

"Shut your trap, Célestin," growled the skipper.

Delcourt was stumping up and down the quay to keep himself warm; also perhaps to keep himself in countenance. He was doubtful whether to move off or stay.

"Tell me, Louis. What made you think that Joris was in danger?"

Louis shrugged his shoulders.

"Eh, man, wouldn't any fool 'a' tumbled to it? Seein' as summun had had a go at him already."

He spoke so thickly that one almost needed an interpreter to explain what he was saying.

All were conscious of a feeling of extreme discomfort, an

ominous suspense. Louis turned and gazed in the direction
of Joris's cottage, but nothing could be seen there, not even
a patch of blacker darkness in the gloom.

"Ain't Julie there?" he asked.

"Yes. Are you going to see her?"

He shook his head. A clumsy, bearish gesture.

"Why not?"

"She'll be blubbin', for sure."

He pronounced it "bloobin' "—and in a tone of venomous disgust, the tone of one who cannot stomach the sight
of tears.

Their clothes were sopping. The drizzle was increasing.
Delcourt suggested:

"How about going over there for a drink?"

One of his men spoke up from the darkness.

"They've just closed."

The skipper of the *Saint Michel* said:

"If you gentlemen don't mind coming down to the
cabin . . ."

A quartette: Maigret, Delcourt, Louis, and the skipper,
whose name was Lannec. The cabin was a mere cubby-
hole. A small stove gave off an intense heat. The room was
filled with a warm, damp haze through which the flame
of an oil-lamp hung on gimbals glowed murky red.

Varnished pitchpine walls. An oak table, so gashed and
battered that there was not an inch of level surface left.
Some dirty plates; thick grease-smeared glasses; a half-
bottle of red wine.

On either side a recess, like a cupboard without a door,
let into the wall. In each was a bed: the skipper's and that
of Louis, his mate. Draggled beds with seaboots and
clothing lying on them. A reek of tar, spirits, food, and an
unventilated bedroom—but, above all, the curious, undefin-
able smell peculiar to ships.

Seen by lamplight, the men looked less sinister. Lannec had a brown mustache and bright shrewd eyes. He had taken a bottle of spirits from a locker and was rinsing out the glasses, emptying them on the floor.

"So you were here on the night of September 16?"

Louis was resting his elbows on the table, his back hunched. Lannec answered, as he handed round the bottle.

"Aye, we were here."

"It's unusual, isn't it, for you to stay the night in the outer harbor, where you have to watch your moorings on account of the tide?"

"We do it sometimes," said Lannec calmly.

"It often saves a few hours in the morning," Delcourt explained. He seemed bent on playing the part of mediator.

"Did Captain Joris come to see you on board?"

"While we were in the lock, yes. Not afterwards."

"And you didn't see or hear anything unusual?"

"Good health, sir! . . . No, nothing."

"You, Louis—did you go to bed?"

"Expect so."

"What do you mean by that?"

"I mean, I s'pose I did. It's so long ago."

"Didn't you go to see your sister?"

"May have done. Not for long, anyhow."

"Hadn't Joris forbidden you to set foot in his house?"

"That's all my eye!"

"What do you mean?"

"Nothing. It's all just bloody nonsense. . . . Well, ain't you done with me?"

There really was no case against the man. And, anyhow, Maigret had not the least wish to arrest him at this stage.

"For the present, yes," he replied.

Louis said some words in Breton to his skipper, rose, drank off his glass, touched his cap.

"What did he say to you?" Maigret asked.

"That I won't need him on the run to Caen and back. He'll meet me here when I've unloaded our cargo."

"Where's he going now?"

"He didn't say."

Delcourt rose hastily, put his head through the hatchway, listened a few minutes, then stepped down again.

"He's on board the dredger."

"The dredger?"

"Didn't you notice the two dredgers moored in the canal? They're not in use just now. Sailors would rather sleep on an old boat than go to a hotel."

"Have another!" Lannec held out the bottle.

Maigret took a quick look round him, screwing up his eyes, then sank back into his chair.

"Tell me. What was the first place you called at after leaving Ouistreham on the sixteenth of last month?"

"Southampton. We were carrying stone."

"Next?"

"Boulogne."

"You didn't go to Norway after that?"

"Only been there once, six years ago."

"Did you know Joris well?"

"Well? Like we know everyone from La Rochelle to Rotterdam, if you see what I mean. Here's the best! This Hollands you're drinking, I brought it back from Rotterdam. Like a cigar?" He took a box from a drawer. "These cigars cost ten cents over there. Only a franc. Good value!"

Fat, well-rolled cigars with gold bands.

"Well, I just can't make it out," sighed Maigret. "I've been assured that Joris went to see you when you were in the outer port—and he had someone with him."

Lannec was busy cutting the tip of a cigar. When he looked up his face was expressionless.

"I've nothing to hide. I'd have told you if he had."

A thud on the deck above. Someone had jumped on to it. A head appeared in the hatchway. "Havre boat sighted."

Delcourt sprang up.

"I must get the lock clear for her. The *Saint Michel* will have to move now."

Lannec turned to the Inspector.

"Anything against my moving on?"

"To Caen?"

"Yes. The canal don't go no farther. I reckon we'll have got our cargo off by tomorrow evening."

All these men had sounded perfectly straightforward, they had an honest air. Yet somehow everything they said rang false. But in so subtle a way that Maigret would have been hard put to it to say what gave him this impression, or where the lies began. Decent fellows, to all appearance. Lannec no less than Delcourt, or Joris, or all the men who forgathered at the *Sailors' Rest*. Even Big Louis, scoundrel though he looked, had something likable about him. . . .

"I'll let go for you, Lannec. Don't move." The harbor-master went up the ladder and cast off the hawser from the bollard.

The old man who had bobbed up from the fo'c'sle shambled across the deck, grumbling: "Blast that Louis! Always clearing off when he's wanted!" After setting the jib and flying jib, he shoved the schooner off with a boat-hook.

Maigret jumped on shore at the last moment. The fog had definitely turned to rain and he now could see the harbor lights, men moving to and fro, and the Havre steamer, which was whistling impatiently outside the lock.

Winches clanked; water began flowing through the sluices. The schooner's mainsail blocked the view up the canal.

Maigret went on to the lock-bridge; thence he had a glimpse of two dredgers—monstrous contraptions, their complicated upper works all caked with rust—made fast to the bank. He picked his way towards them; the ground was littered with rubbish of all sorts: rusty cables, anchors, scrap-iron. Crossing by a plank that served as gangway, he noticed a light showing through a chink.

"Louis!" he called.

The light went out at once. Louis's head and shoulders emerged from a hatch, the lid of which had been removed.

"Whatcher want?" he snarled.

Just then something moved beneath him, in the belly of the dredger. Someone was groping about in the darkness below. There was a muffled clang, as if he had stumbled against a steel plate.

"Who's on board with you?"

"Dunno!"

Maigret started moving forward, tripped and nearly fell into the bilge, where mud lay three feet deep. He could still hear someone creeping gingerly about, but the sounds now came from the far end of the ship. And after bumping his head against a bucket he realized that the way there might be strewn with pitfalls; this type of craft was a complete mystery to him.

"So you refuse to speak?"

The answer was a grunting noise, which seemed to convey: "Dunno whatcher talking about!"

To search the two dredgers thoroughly on a pitch-dark night like this would require ten men at least—and men familiar with them at that. Hopeless! Maigret retreated along the gang-plank. Voices were carrying well because of the rain, and he heard someone saying at the lock:

"It lay right across the fairway."

Walking on, he found the man who had spoken, the

second officer on the Havre steamer, pointing out something to Delcourt. The harbor-master seemed badly flustered at seeing Maigret there.

"I don't see how they could have lost it without noticing," the second officer went on.

"Lost what?" Maigret asked.

"The boat."

"What boat?"

"This one. We ran into it just now, between the jetties. It belongs to the schooner ahead of us. The name's on the stern: *Saint Michel.*"

"Must have worked loose somehow," Delcourt suggested in a casual tone. "That often happens."

"No, it can't have worked loose, for the simple reason that, with the weather as it is, the schooner can't have had the boat in tow, but on deck."

Once again there was a tension in the air: all the lockhands at their posts listening with all their ears.

"I'll attend to it tomorrow. Leave the boat here." Turning to Maigret, Delcourt added with a rather forced smile: "Curious job, a harbor-master's, isn't it? Always something cropping up."

The Inspector, however, did not smile, and his tone was grave as he said:

"Listen! If you don't see me tomorrow morning at seven—well, let's say eight—please ring up the Public Prosecutor at Caen."

"What on earth . . . ?"

"Good night. And see that boat stays here, please."

To throw dust in their eyes, he started walking along the jetty, his hands in his pockets, the collar of his coat turned up. Waves were crashing against the breakwaters; the breeze was strongly charged with ozone.

Near the end of the jetty he stooped and picked something up.

5. *Notre-Dame des Dunes*

AT sunrise Maigret returned to the *Hôtel de l'Univers*. His overcoat was soaked through, his throat parched by a night's incessant smoking. At the hotel no one seemed to be up. In the kitchen, however, he discovered the hotelkeeper, lighting the fire.

"So you stayed out all night?"

"Yes. Would you bring some coffee to my room as soon as possible? Any chance of a bath?"

"I'll have to light the furnace."

"Don't bother."

A gray morning. The inevitable fog—but a paler, lighter fog than usual. Maigret's eyes smarted, his head felt like a hollow block of wood. He opened the window and sat in front of it, waiting for his coffee.

A curious night it had been. He'd done nothing sensational, made no startling discovery. Yet he'd come a step nearer understanding the problem. Several new facts had swelled the total of his knowledge.

The coming of the *Saint Michel* and Lannec's behavior. Suspicious? No, that wasn't the word. Shifty. Lacking frankness. Delcourt, too, seemed to be keeping something back at times. So did they all, for that matter, every manjack of them!

Louis's attitude, on the other hand, was definitely suspicious. He had not gone with the schooner to Caen. He had spent the night on a disused dredger and, Maigret was positive, he hadn't been alone on board.

Then there was the business of the *Saint Michel's* boat,

found adrift at the entrance of the harbor. And at the end of the jetty the Inspector had picked up something most unlikely to be found at that particular place: a gold fountain-pen.

The jetty was a wooden structure, built on piles. At the end, beside the green light, an iron ladder led down to the sea. The boat had been found near by. The inference was obvious. The *Saint Michel* had brought a passenger who did not wish to be seen in Ouistreham. He had landed from the boat and let it drift away. At the top of the ladder, as he was hoisting himself on to the jetty, the gold fountain-pen had slipped from his pocket. Then he had proceeded to the dredger, where Louis had gone to join him.

There was no alternative explanation; this sequence of events was proved with almost mathematical certainty.

It followed that an unknown man was lying low at Ouistreham. He had not come here for nothing; he had certainly some scheme in mind. And he belonged to a social *milieu* in which gold fountain-pens were used.

Not a sailor, then; not a tramp. Well-to-do; presumably well dressed. A "dude" the countryfolk would call him. And in winter, at Ouistreham, a "dude" was bound to attract attention. He wouldn't dare to leave the dredger by daylight. Whatever he was out to do would be done by night.

So Maigret, as in duty bound, had kept watch all night. A junior officer's job. Hour after dreary hour, under the drizzle, he had peered into the dark recesses of the dredger. Nothing had happened. No one had come ashore. Dawn had risen on his fruitless vigil. And, as the last straw, the hot bath he had been counting on was not forthcoming! His eyes fell on the bed. How about a few hours' sleep?

The hotel-keeper brought the coffee.

"Aren't you going to bed?"

"Maybe. . . . Would you take a telegram to the post-office?"

A wire to Lucas, his assistant, to come at once. Maigret did not relish the prospect of another night's sentry-go beside the canal.

The window overlooked the harbor, Joris's cottage, the sand-banks in the bay that the ebb was now disclosing. As Maigret scribbled the telegram the hotel-keeper was gazing out of the window. Casually he remarked:

"Hullo! There's the Captain's servant going for a walk."

The Inspector looked quickly around. He saw Julie close the garden gate and start off at a quick pace towards the beach.

"What's over there?"

"I don't follow."

"I mean, where can she be going? Are there any houses in that direction?"

"None at all. It's just bare beach, and no one uses it, because it's cut up by breakwaters and mud-holes."

"There's no road or path?"

"No. You come to the mouth of the Orne, and there's nothing but marshes along the bank. Wait a bit! There are some pits dug in the marshes which are used for duck-shooting."

Maigret was already on his feet. His brows were knitted. He strode rapidly across the bridge; when he reached the beach, Julie was only a couple of hundred yards ahead of him.

Nobody was about. No sign of life along the foreshore, except the sea-gulls wheeling and wailing overhead. On the right was a line of dunes; the Inspector turned off amongst them, so as not to be seen.

The air was brisk, the sea smooth. Only a thin ribbon of white foam lapped the shore, with a low rustle of shells and shingle.

Obviously Julie was not out for a mere stroll. She walked quickly, holding her small black coat tightly wrapped about her. There had been no time since Joris's death to buy mourning, so she had fallen back on the darkest garments she possessed—that old-fashioned coat, a cloche hat, gray woolen stockings.

She moved in jerks, as her feet stuck in the loose sand. Twice she looked back, but failed to see Maigret, who was hidden by the sand-hills.

At last, about a mile from Ouistreham, she swerved off to the right—so abruptly that the Inspector all but let himself be seen. His first idea was that she must be making for a shooting-pit. But in the wide expanse of rank grass and sand there was no sign of human life.

Only a small decrepit building, one wall missing, that faced the sea, some five yards inland from high-water mark. There, centuries ago, most likely, pious hands had built a little chapel.

There was a vaulted roof, and the gap in the walls enabled Maigret to gauge their thickness, a yard or so of solid stone.

After entering the chapel, Julie walked to the far end; and at once Maigret heard a rustle of small objects being displaced—sea-shells, judging by the sound.

He crept forward. In the eastward wall was a small railed-off recess. Beneath it a sort of tiny altar. Julie was stooping, hunting for something.

Suddenly she looked up. The Inspector had no time to take cover.

"What are you doing here?" she cried.

"What are *you* doing?"

"I . . . I've come to pray to Our Lady of the Dunes."

She was obviously worried. Her whole demeanor showed that she had something to hide. Evidently she had passed an almost sleepless night, for her eyes were bloodshot. She had dressed in haste; two wisps of hair straggled out under the brim of her hat.

"Ah! So this place is dedicated to Our Lady of the Dunes."

Looking more carefully, he descried behind the bars a statue of the Virgin, but so worn and worm-eaten as to be almost shapeless. Round the little shrine was a jumble of inscriptions cut in the stone with penknives or pointed stones, or scribbled in pencil:

"Please make Denise pass her exam." "Please, Our Lady, may little Joey learn to read soon." "Please give good health to all the family, especially poor Grandpa and Grandmama." Less devout inscriptions, too. Hearts pierced by arrows. *"True lovers, Bob and Jeanne."*

Shreds of what had once been flowers still clung to the railing. But what made the chapel different from others was a pyramid of shells on the small tumbledown altar.

On each something was written, usually in pencil —in childish or illiterate writing for the most part. *"May they have a good catch in Newfoundland so that dad needn't go to sea again."*

The floor was of beaten earth. Through the gap in the walls one saw a stretch of golden sand, a silver expanse of sea shimmering in the morning light. Julie kept eyeing apprehensively the heap of shells, though she tried not to look in that direction.

"Did you bring one?" Maigret asked.

She shook her head.

"But just before I came you were moving them about. What were you looking for?"

"Nothing. I only . . ." She paused.

"Yes?"

"Oh, nothing." An obstinate look had settled on her face. She wrapped her coat more tightly round her.

Maigret decided to examine the shells one by one. Suddenly he smiled. On a big clam-shell he had read: *"Our Lady of the Dunes, please may my brother Louis bring it off and all of us be happy."* It bore a date: *"September 13."* . . . So this rustic votive offering had been placed here three days before Joris disappeared.

Probably Julie had come here to retrieve it.

"This is what you were looking for, isn't it?"

"That's my business!"

She stared at the shell. She seemed on the point of making a rush at Maigret, snatching it from his hand.

"Give it back to me. Put it back where you found it."

"All right, I'll put it back—but, mind, you've got to leave it here. Come along now. We'll have a talk on the way home."

"I've nothing to tell you."

Their feet sank into the sand and they leant forward as they walked. A cold wind nipped their cheeks, reddened their noses.

"Your brother's always been a bit of a ne'er-do-well, eh?" No reply. She was staring straight in front of her, along the beach. "There's some things," Maigret went on, "that it's no good trying to conceal. I don't mean only that . . . that Louis fell foul of the law on one occasion."

"You've said it!" she broke in. "My brother's a jailbird. Twenty years from now they'll still be throwing it up at me."

"No, Julie, that's not what I meant. Louis is a fine sailor. First-rate at his job, so I've been told. Good enough to act as captain's mate. Only—at times he gets into bad

company, drinks too much and paints the town red. Then,
instead of going back to his ship, he loafs about for weeks
on end, doing nothing. When all his money's gone he
comes to you for help. On one occasion, some weeks ago,
he asked Joris to help him out. When the drinking bout is
over he settles down again and does another spell of honest work."

"Well?"

"What was it that on the thirteenth of September you
wanted Louis to 'bring off'?"

She stopped walking and looked him in the face. She had
had time to think things out and was much calmer now.
There was a charming gravity in the young eyes.

"Somehow I knew it would mean trouble for us all.
But my brother hasn't done anything wrong. I swear to
you that if he'd killed the Captain I'd have been the first
to see he got what he deserved." Her voice had an under-
tone of strong emotion. "It's just bad luck that things look
black against him. And, of course, his being a 'jailbird.'
Catch people forgetting that! Whenever anyone does anything wrong at Ouistreham, they try to fasten it on him."

"What was Louis's plan?"

"It wasn't what I'd call a plan. Something quite simple
really. He'd met a very rich gentleman—at Havre or in
England, I don't know which. He never told me his name.
This gentleman had taken it into his head to buy a yacht.
He'd had enough of life on shore and wanted to go for
cruises. He asked Louis to look round for a boat for him."

They were still standing on the beach. All that could be
seen of Ouistreham was a white tower outlined against a
still paler sky—the lighthouse.

"Louis talked to his boss about it. There's been a slump,
you know, and Lannec wanted to sell his schooner. The
Saint Michel's just the sort of craft that could be easily

converted into a yacht. My brother was to get ten thousand francs if the deal came off. What's more, the buyer talked of taking him on as skipper; he wanted somebody reliable."

She shot a quick glance at Maigret, conscious that she had blundered in using the word "reliable" of an ex-convict, and half expecting to see an ironic smile on his lips.

But there was not the ghost of a smile. Maigret was pondering deeply. He was impressed by the straightforwardness of her story; it had the ring of truth.

"So you can't tell me the name of the man who wanted to buy the *Saint Michel?*"

"No."

"Where was your brother to meet him?"

"I don't know."

"When?"

"Quite soon. Louis told me that the alterations were to be made in Norway. In a month's time they'd be off on their first voyage. To Egypt, he said."

"Was the man a Frenchman?"

"I don't know."

"You came to the chapel today to take away your shell, didn't you?"

"Well, I thought that if someone found it it might give them . . . wrong ideas. . . . You don't believe a word of what I'm saying, do you?"

Maigret made as if he had not heard, and asked:

"Seen your brother?"

She gave a start. "When?"

"Last night, or this morning?"

"What? Is Louis here?" She sounded at once alarmed and puzzled.

"The *Saint Michel*'s in."

This, apparently, reassured her somewhat; it looked as

if she'd been afraid her brother might turn up without his ship.

"I suppose he's gone on to Caen," she said.

"No. He spent the night on board one of the dredgers."

"Let's walk," she said. "It's cold standing about."

The sky was getting overcast, the sea-wind freshening.

"Does he often spend the night like that, on a laid-up ship?"

No answer. Neither seemed to have any more to say. The only sound was the crunch of sand under their feet and the light patter of sea-lice hopping away from their meal on the seaweed cast up by the tide.

Two pictures were linking up in Maigret's mind. A yacht; a gold fountain-pen. The link formed almost automatically. Till now the gold fountain-pen had been a puzzle; it didn't fit in with the *Saint Michel* and her rather rapscallion crew. But a yacht—that was another story. A well-to-do, middle-aged man looking for a yacht to cruise about in might very well possess a gold fountain-pen, and lose it.

However, there remained an element of mystery. Why on earth should the man, instead of coming with the schooner into port, have landed from the ship's boat at the end of the jetty, and then slunk off to hide in a more or less water-logged dredger?

"When your brother came to see you on the night before Joris disappeared, did he say anything about the man who wanted to buy the schooner? Did he tell you, for instance, that the man was on board?"

"No, he simply said the deal was practically fixed up."

They were walking past the lighthouse. Joris's cottage was on their left; flowers that he had planted in the garden were still in bloom.

Julie's face clouded over; she cast a listless glance around, as if she had lost interest in life.

"The lawyer will be sending for you to hear the Will, I expect. You're a rich woman now."

"Nothing doing!" she said curtly.

"What do you mean?"

"You can't bamboozle me. The Captain wasn't at all well off. I know it as well as you do."

"How can you be sure?"

"He told me everything. If he'd had a pile, I'd have known it. Do you know, last winter he couldn't bring himself to spend three thousand francs on a shot-gun. And I know he was awfully keen on getting it. He'd seen the mayor's and asked how much it cost." They had reached the garden gate. "Won't you step inside?"

"No. But I may look in later."

She was obviously reluctant to enter the lonely cottage. . . .

The next two hours passed uneventfully. Maigret prowled round the dredger like a tripper eyeing respectfully a big machine whose monstrous gadgets—curly iron pipes, buckets, chains, and capstans—fascinate and mystify him.

By eleven he was back in the harbor, having a drink with the men from the lock.

"Anyone seen Big Louis?"

Yes, he had been seen, quite early in the morning. He had had two glasses of rum, then started off along the high road.

Maigret felt half asleep. Had he caught a chill last night? he wondered. Certainly he had all the symptoms of a man who's in for a bad cold. And this betrayed itself in his movements and his eyes, which had lost their usual alertness.

He took no trouble to conceal his discomfort, and it made the men around him still more ill at ease. They shot stealthy glances at him. Conversation flagged. At last Delcourt asked:

"What shall I do with the boat?"

"Oh, tie it up somewhere."

Then Maigret put a rather clumsy question:

"Has anyone here seen a stranger about in the village this morning? Or anything unusual happening near the dredgers?"

No, no one had noticed anything. But his words had a curious effect. Now he had suggested it, everybody expected to see something! A sort of collective hunch—that sensational developments were at hand! The cycle of events was not yet closed. A link was missing still.

A steamer hooted for the lock-gates to open. Everyone rose. Maigret trudged wearily to the post-office to see if there was anything for him. Only a wire from Lucas to say he was arriving at 2.10. . . .

Punctually the diminutive train—like a child's toy, with carriages built on the 1850 model—that plies along the canal-bank between Caen and Ouistreham, fussed in, puffing and blowing, with a squeal of antiquated brakes.

As Lucas alighted and held out his hand, he was startled by Maigret's look of gloom.

"What's the matter?"

"I'm all right."

Lucas forgot his normal deference and laughed outright.

"Well, you certainly don't look it. . . . By the way, I haven't lunched."

"Come along to the hotel. They'll dig up something for you."

While Lucas had a hasty meal in the big dining-room they conversed in undertones. The proprietor hovered round, evidently anxious to put in a word.

At last, as he served the cheese, he judged the moment had come.

"Have you heard what's happened to the mayor?"

Maigret gave a start, and he looked so alarmed that the man made haste to add:

"Oh, it's nothing serious. I hear he had a fall when he was coming downstairs this morning. Nobody seems to know exactly what happened, but he knocked his face about so badly that he's had to take to his bed."

Then Maigret had an inspiration. The word is not too strong, for it was in a flash that his lively imagination visualized the incident.

"Is Madame Grandmaison still at Ouistreham?"

"No, she left this morning with her daughter. I expect she's gone to Caen. She took the car."

Maigret's incipient cold had vanished as if by magic.

"Aren't you *ever* going to finish your lunch, Lucas?"

"All in good time," Lucas rejoined imperturbably. "I dare say when a chap's had his fill already, the sight of another fellow tucking in is pretty revolting. . . . Anyhow, three minutes more will do me . . . No, don't take the Camembert away yet," he added, to the hotel-keeper.

6. *The Mayor's Mishap*

THE news, as transmitted by the proprietor of the hotel, was certainly exaggerated. Monsieur Grandmaison was not in bed. So much Maigret discovered for himself at once when, after sending Lucas to keep watch on the dredger, he walked to the mayor's house. From the road he could see beside the biggest window a form, slumped in the time-honored attitude of convalescence, in an armchair.

Undoubtedly the mayor; though the man's features could not be clearly seen.

There was someone else in the room, standing farther back from the window. His face, too, could not be made out.

When Maigret rang there was more commotion inside the house than is usual when a caller arrives. At last a maid appeared; an elderly, rather sour-faced woman. Evidently she had a profound disdain for visitors as a class, for she did not deign so much as to open her lips.

She pointed to the short flight of steps leading to the hall, leaving Maigret to close the door after him. Then she knocked at a double door and stood aside while Maigret entered the study, unannounced.

There was something peculiar about the whole proceedings. Nothing sensationally so, but a host of small details that seemed out of keeping, a slightly abnormal atmosphere.

The house was the ordinary type of French seaside house, but exceptionally spacious and almost new. Still, considering how rich the Grandmaisons were, owning as they did the bulk of the shares in the Anglo-Norman Line, there was less display of luxury than one would have expected.

Perhaps, Maigret surmised, they spent their money on the residence at Caen.

He had moved only a few steps into the room when a voice hailed him, from beside the window.

"Who's there? Oh, it's you, Inspector!"

Monsieur Grandmaison was reclining in a big hide armchair, his legs propped on another chair. As he was between Maigret and the light it was hard to see him clearly, but the Inspector noticed that he was wearing a scarf knotted round his neck instead of a collar, and masking his left cheek with his hand.

"Sit down."

Maigret walked round the room, and drew a chair up facing the shipowner. He had some trouble in repressing a smile, so amazing was the sight confronting him. Monsieur Grandmaison's left cheek—he was unable to cover it completely with his hand—was swollen, so was his upper lip. But what the mayor was trying above all to conceal was an enormous black eye!

The spectacle would not have been so comical had not the great man been trying so hard to keep his dignity intact. He did not flinch, but glared at Maigret suspiciously.

"I presume you've come to report the results of your inquiry?"

"No; this is a sort of duty call. I appreciated so much the cordiality with which you received me the other day that I felt it up to me to call and thank you." Maigret never indulged in sarcastic smiles; on the contrary, the more ironical he was, the graver his expression.

Meanwhile his eyes were exploring the study. On the walls hung structural plans of cargo-boats and photographs of the Company's steamers. The furniture was strictly business-like: plain mahogany. On the desk lay some files, letters, and telegrams. The floor was highly polished. The Inspector's eyes lingered on it with marked satisfaction.

"I hear you've had an accident."

The mayor sighed, shifted his legs, and muttered:

"I slipped coming down the stairs."

"This morning, wasn't it? It must have given Madame Grandmaison a nasty shock."

"My wife had left when it happened."

"Ah, yes, of course. It's not the time of year for staying at the seaside. Unless one's keen on duck-shooting. Madame Grandmaison's gone back to Caen with your daughter, I suppose?"

"No. To Paris."

A gray flannel shirt, dark trousers, carpet slippers, an old dressing-gown. . . . This morning the shipowner had none of his usual spruceness.

"What was there at the foot of the stairs?"

"What do you mean?"

"I mean, what did you fall on?"

A venomous glance; then the mayor replied:

"Why, on the floor, of course."

A transparent lie. A man couldn't get a black eye like that by falling on the floor. Nor those tell-tale marks of clutching fingers round his throat.

When the scarf moved the merest fraction of an inch, Maigret clearly saw the bruises it was intended to hide.

"You were alone in the house, of course?"

"Why 'of course'?"

"Well, accidents have a way of happening when there's nobody about."

"The maid was out doing her marketing."

"Is she the only servant here?"

"There's the gardener. But he's gone to Caen today, shopping."

"It must have been a very disagreeable experience."

What, above all, baffled the mayor was Maigret's imperturbable gravity; he sounded genuinely concerned.

It was only half-past three, but dusk was falling already, the room getting dark. Maigret's hand went to his pocket.

"You don't mind if I smoke a pipe?"

"If you prefer a cigar, you'll find some on the mantelpiece."

On a tray stood a bottle of Armagnac. A pile of packing-cases in a corner. Tall doors in plain, polished deal.

"How's your investigation getting on?" the mayor inquired.

Maigret made an evasive gesture. He was keeping a hold on himself to prevent his eyes from straying to the door leading into the next room, the drawing-room. The door was vibrating in a most peculiar manner.

"No results, eh?" the mayor continued.

"Nothing, so far."

"Like to have my opinion? It was a mistake treating this as a complicated case."

"Obviously," Maigret grunted. "Clear as daylight, isn't it? One night a man disappears, and his movements for a month and more cannot be traced. Six weeks later he turns up in Paris. He's been shot through the head and had his skull patched up. His memory's gone. He is brought home and poisoned that very night. Meanwhile three hundred thousand francs have been paid into his account, from Hamburg. . . . A simple case! Nothing complicated about it!"

The tone was mild, but now there was no mistaking the Inspector's meaning.

"Yes, yes. . . . But all the same, it may be simpler than you think. And even supposing there's some mystery behind it, in my opinion it's a great mistake to go about creating—deliberately creating—feelings of uneasiness in the village. You know how those men are; they drink like fish, their nerves are none too steady at the best of times. If one keeps harping on such matters in the local bars, it may throw them altogether off their balance."

He had spoken slowly, emphatically, with a stern look on his face and in the tone of a committing magistrate.

"On the other hand, no attempt has been made to co-operate with the proper authorities. I, the mayor of the town, haven't a notion what you're up to, down in the harbor."

"Does your gardener wear rope-soled shoes?"

The mayor shot a quick glance at the floor. On the polished surface were foot-prints, the criss-cross patterns of jute soles.

"Haven't a notion."

"Sorry to have interrupted. Just an idea that had occurred to me. What were you saying? . . ."

But the thread of his discourse was broken. Monsieur Grandmaison merely growled:

"Would you hand me that box of cigars on the mantelpiece? Thanks."

As the cigar touched his wounded lip he winced. After a long puff he spoke again.

"Well, how far have you got with the case? You must have gathered *some* information anyhow."

"Nothing to speak of."

"That surprises me. Those chaps down in the harbor aren't lacking in imagination as a rule—especially after a few drinks."

"I suppose you sent Madame Grandmaison to Paris to

get her away from . . . from these unpleasant events. Not to mention those which may still occur."

It was not open warfare, but there was an undercurrent of hostility on both sides. Due, perhaps, merely to the different social classes for which the two men stood. Maigret hobnobbed with fishermen and lock-keepers at the "local"; while the mayor entertained high officials with cups of tea, liqueurs, and fancy cakes.

Maigret was just a man—without the "guinea stamp." Whereas Monsieur Grandmaison had an assured position, he was the typical small-town magnate, member of a well-established upper middle-class family, not to mention the owner of a flourishing shipping concern.

True, he affected a democratic manner, was hail-fellow-well-met with all around him. But his geniality was patronizing; put on to curry favor with voters.

There was something formidable about Maigret's stolid tenacity, and Monsieur Grandmaison was rapidly dropping his domineering manner, showing signs of uneasiness. Now, in a last attempt to regain the whip-hand of the conversation, he adopted an angry tone.

"Monsieur Maigret"—the way he said the words was a masterpiece of haughty condescension—"Monsieur Maigret, permit me to remind you that as the mayor of this township . . ."

The Inspector rose—so casually that the mayor could only gaze at him in sheer surprise—walked up to a door and opened it.

"Do come in, Louis! It's getting on my nerves, seeing that door shaking all the time and hearing you puffing like a grampus just behind it."

If Maigret had expected a dramatic scene to follow, he was disappointed. "Big Louis" did as he was told, slouched into the study, and halted, staring glumly at the floor. But it was more the attitude of someone in a quandary than that of a rough sailor ill at ease in the magnificence of a rich man's home.

The mayor puffed furiously at his cigar, gazing straight in front of him.

Dusk had fallen in the room. A gas-lamp was already lit in the street.

"May I turn on the light?" Maigret asked.

"Yes. But draw the curtains first. There's no need for all the passers-by to . . . No. The pull's on the left-hand side. Gently. . . ."

Louis remained standing in the middle of the room, unmoving. Maigret switched on the lights, walked over to the stove and gave it a poke. A habit he had, like his habit of standing on the hearthrug, his hands behind him, toasting his back.

Had the situation changed in any way? There was now a glint of mockery in Monsieur Grandmaison's eyes as he watched the Inspector, who was lost in thought.

"Was Louis here at the time of your . . . accident?"

An emphatic "No!"

"That's just too bad! It might have accounted . . . Well, for instance, when you fell downstairs, your face might have landed on his fist. . . ."

"Yes, and it would have given you another pretext for starting all sorts of crazy rumors and making the poor fellows in the pubs even more jumpy than they are already! . . . I suggest, Inspector, that we've wasted enough time beating about the bush. There are two of us, don't forget; two of us on this case. How do things stand? You came here from Paris. You brought Captain Joris with you. He was in a pitiable state, and everything goes to show it wasn't here, at Ouistreham, he got his injury. You were here when he was killed. You're conducting this inquiry as you think fit. That's your affair. But don't forget"—his voice was authoritative—"don't forget I've been mayor of this place for nearly ten years. I know the people here and I consider myself responsible for anything that affects their safety. As mayor, I am also head of the local police. Well then . . ." He paused to take a long puff at his cigar; the ash fell, spraying his dressing-gown with gray flakes. "While you've been haunting the local pubs, I've been putting in some work on this case myself—though you may be surprised to hear it."

"And you sent for Louis in the course of your inquiry?"

"I shall send for others, too, if I think fit. . . . Well, I suppose you've nothing more to tell me? No?"

He rose, rather stiffly, to see his visitor to the door.

"I hope," said Maigret quietly, "that you've no objection to my taking Louis with me. I questioned him last night, but there are a few more things I'd like to ask him."

Monsieur Grandmaison's gesture signified that he had no objection. Louis, however, didn't budge, but remained staring bemusedly at the floor.

"Are you coming, Louis?"

"Nao! Ain't a-comin' yet," he muttered in his usual bearish growl.

"Please take note," the mayor put in, "that I've raised no obstacle to his going with you. I draw your attention to this in case you should accuse me of trying to hamper your inquiry. I sent for Louis as I wanted information from him on certain matters. If he chooses to stay, it's presumably because he has something more to tell."

All the same, there was now a sense of apprehension in the air—not merely in the air, and more than apprehension. For it was almost panic that Maigret glimpsed in the mayor's eyes.

Louis's lips parted in a grin of bestial satisfaction.

"I'll wait for you outside," said the Inspector.

Louis kept silence. It was the mayor who spoke.

"Then, *au revoir*, Inspector Maigret."

As Maigret left the room the maid came hastily from the kitchen; silent and surly as ever, she showed him out and shut the door behind him.

The road was empty. A hundred yards away, a light showed at a window. Beyond it other lights, spaced out at longish intervals, for the houses in Riva Bella Road are surrounded by good-sized gardens.

Maigret walked slowly to the garden gate, his back hunched, his hands in his overcoat pockets. Facing him was a stretch of waste land. This part of Ouistreham is built along the edge of the dunes, and between the gardens and the sea is a strip of sand and stunted grass.

A shadow in the dusk. A voice.

"That you, Inspector?"

"Lucas?"

Each made a quick step forward.

"Why are you here?"

His eyes still fixed on the garden, Lucas whispered:

"The man from the dredger."

"Has he left it?"

"He's here."

"How long has he been here?"

"Barely a quarter of an hour. He's just behind the house."

"Inside the railings?"

"No. . . . He seems to be waiting for someone. I heard your footsteps. So I came to tell you."

"Show me where he is."

Skirting the garden, they came out at the back of the house. Lucas muttered: "Damn!"

"What's up?"

"He's gone."

"Sure?"

"He was standing by that clump of tamarisks."

"Think he's entered the house?"

"Haven't a notion."

"Stop here. Don't move for any reason whatsoever."

Maigret ran back to the road. No one in sight. A strip of light showed through the study window, but the window-ledge was out of reach.

He made up his mind. Crossing the garden, he rang the bell. The maid opened almost at once.

"I think I left my pipe in the study."

"I'll go and see."

She left him standing at the door. No sooner was she out of sight than he ran up the stairs on tiptoe and peeped into the study.

The mayor was sitting in the same place, his legs stretched in front of him. A small table had been placed beside his chair. Louis was seated on the other side of the table.

Between them was a draught-board. The sailor moved a piece, then rumbled:

"Your turn."

As the mayor watched the maid hunting for the pipe, his nerves were obviously on edge. At last he broke out:

"You can see for yourself it isn't here. Tell the Inspector he must have dropped it on the road. . . . Your move, Louis."

Quite at home, Louis turned to the maid.

"Bring us some drinks, Marguerite, while you're about it."

7. Maigret Sets the Pace

"THINGS are going to hum!" thought Lucas when he saw the look on Maigret's face as he left the house. "Primed up, he is! I know the signs." The Inspector was gazing straight in front of him, with seemingly unseeing eyes.

"Wasn't he in the house?"

"No, and it's no use wasting our time over him. We'd need a dozen men at least to round up a fellow hiding in the dunes."

His overcoat buttoned up to the neck, his hands thrust deep in his pockets, Maigret was chewing the stem of his pipe.

"See that chink between the curtains?" he said, pointing to the study window. "And that low wall just in front? I rather think that if you got on to the wall you could see into the room."

Lucas was almost as burly as Maigret, but a little shorter. With a sigh he scrambled up the wall, after a quick glance down the road in each direction to make sure no one was about.

A wind had sprung up with the nightfall; a sea-wind that grew stronger every minute and whistled through the trees.

"Can you see in?"

"The wall's a bit too low. Another six or eight inches and I'd manage it."

Without replying, Maigret crossed the road to a stone-heap he had noticed, fetched some big stones and put them on the wall.

"That better?"

"I can see the edge of the table now, but I can't see their faces."

Maigret fetched some more stones.

"That's done it. They're playing draughts. The maid's come in with hot drinks of some kind—grog, I should say."

"Stay where you are."

Maigret fell to pacing up and down the road. A hundred yards away was the *Sailors' Rest;* beyond it the harbor. A baker's van came up the road. He was in half a mind to stop it and make sure no one was hidden inside—but dismissed the project with a shrug. Some police operations look quite simple, but don't work out in practice. For instance, a search for the man who had been behind the mayor's house. One would have to scour the dunes, the beach, the village, and the harbor; to have the roads patrolled. Why, a whole squad of police wouldn't be enough! And, even so, if the man kept his wits about him, he'd slip through their fingers.

Moreover, he, Maigret, had no idea who the man was or what he looked like.

He walked back to the wall on which Lucas was still keeping uncomfortable watch.

"What are they doing?"

"Still playing draughts."

"Talking?"

"No, neither has said a word. That convict fellow has his elbows on the table and is at his third grog already."

A quarter of an hour passed. Then they heard the buzz of an electric bell inside the house.

"A telephone call," Lucas said. "The mayor's getting

up. No, Louis is lifting the receiver. . . . Louis is hang-ing up. Looks pleased with himself. . . . They're at their game again."

"Stay here," Maigret said; then walked rapidly towards the café.

There was the usual group of card-players. They asked Maigret to join them in a drink.

"Not just now, thanks. . . . Is there a telephone here, mademoiselle?"

The telephone was in the kitchen, where an old woman was busy cleaning fish.

"Hullo! Ouistreham post-office? Police here. Tell me, who called up the mayor just now?"

"The call was from Caen, sir."

"Number?"

"122. The *Café de la Gare*."

"Thanks." He hung up and went out.

For a moment he stood motionless in the middle of the public room, oblivious of all around him. "It's seven miles from here to Caen." Unknowingly he had said it aloud.

"Eight," amended Captain Delcourt, who had just come in. "How are you, Inspector?"

But Maigret did not hear. "On a bike, say half an hour," he murmured.

He remembered that most of the men working at the lock lived in the village and came to their work on bi-cycles, which they parked in a shelter opposite the café.

"Please go out and see if all your bicycles are there."

From now on, everything went like clockwork. Maigret's brain worked like a cogwheel geared to the sequence of events.

"Hell! My bike's not there!"

He was not surprised, asked for no details, but walked back to the kitchen and lifted the receiver.

"Police station, Caen, please. Thank you. Is that the central police station? Inspector Maigret speaking—yes, Maigret of the *P.J.* Is there a train to Paris leaving soon? What? Not before eleven? Listen! Please take this down. I'll number the points.

"One. Find out if Madame Grandmaison—yes, the shipowner's wife—has really gone to Paris in her car.

"Two. Has any stranger visited Grandmaison's house, or office, today? Yes, yes. That should be easy. Wait, that's not all. You're taking it down, aren't you?

"Three. Have inquiries made at all garages. How many are there at Caen? Twenty? Wait! Only the garages that let out cars concern us. Begin with the ones near the station. Right! Find out if anyone has just hired a car, with or without a driver, to go to Paris. Or has just bought a second-hand car. Hullo! Hold the line, damn it! He may have dumped a bike at Caen. Find out!

"Yes, that's all. Have you enough men to send on all these three inquiries right away? O.K. The moment you have any news, ring me up at the *Sailors' Rest*, Ouistreham. Got it? Right!"

In the café they had heard every word. When Maigret came back into the room everyone was looking badly rattled.

"About my bike," one of them began timidly. "Do you think—?"

But Maigret took no notice. Calling the waitress, he ordered a hot grog. No longer was he the boon companion of the last few days, who stood his rounds of drinks and joined in theirs. It was as if he hardly saw them, had never met them.

"Is the *Saint Michel* back from Caen?"

"She's due in for tonight's tide. But she mayn't be able to go out with the weather as it is."

"A storm?"

"A stiff gale of wind, anyhow. And it's veering north—which is a bad sign hereabouts. Hear it?"

Listening, Maigret heard a sound like a drum beating in the distance, waves breaking on the piles of the jetty. A violent gust rattled the door.

"If there's a ring for me, send someone to let me know at once. I'll be on the road, about a hundred yards from here."

"Outside the mayor's?"

It was all Maigret could do to light his pipe once he was outside. Low, ragged clouds were racing across the sky, seeming to catch in the top branches of the poplars that lined the road. At five yards' distance Sergeant Lucas, standing on the wall, was almost invisible.

"Anything happened?"

"They've stopped playing draughts. Louis seemed to get sick of the game all of a sudden and swept the pieces off the board."

"What are they up to now?"

"The mayor's lying back in his chair. The sailor man's smoking a cigar and swilling grog. He's torn a dozen cigars to shreds in the last half-hour. From the way he grinned, he did it just to spite the other fellow I should say."

"How many drinks?"

"Five or six."

All Maigret could see was a tiny slit of light in the frontage of the house. Some bricklayers cycling home from their work went by. Then a farm-cart. Vaguely aware of people lurking in the darkness, the driver whipped up his horse and looked round nervously several times after he had passed.

"What about the maid?"

"Haven't seen her again. In the kitchen, I expect. I say, am I to stop here much longer? If so, you might put some more stones on the wall; it's the hell of a strain craning my neck all the time."

Maigret did so. The sound of waves was swelling to a roar. Big waves, six-footers, toppling in cataracts of foam.

A hundred yards down the road a door slammed. Someone came up the road from the *Sailors' Rest,* groping his way. Maigret hastened towards him.

"Ah, there you are. You're wanted on the 'phone."

Caen calling—sooner than he'd expected.

"Hullo? Inspector Maigret? Yes, Madame Grand-maison came to Caen this morning in the car. She left her daughter at her house, with the governess, and started off at noon in the direction of Paris. You were right about the stranger, too. Can't think how you tumbled to it! We found the right garage first shot: the one in front of the station. A man turned up there on a bicycle. He tried to hire a car without a driver. The garage people told him they didn't see their way, and so forth. . . .

"The man seemed in a great hurry. He then asked them to sell him a car, a fast one, second-hand if possible. They let him have one for twenty thousand francs. He paid cash. It's a yellow touring-car, lettered *W,* like all cars for sale."

"Do they know which way he went?"

"He asked for information about the road to Paris, *via* Lisieux and Evreux."

"Ring up the police stations at Lisieux, Evreux, and Mantes. And warn Paris to keep a look-out for this car at all the entrances to the city, especially Porte Maillot."

"Should the car be taken in charge?"

"Yes, and the driver too. You have a description of him, haven't you?"

"The garage-keeper supplied one. A rather tall, middle-aged man, well dressed, wearing a light gray suit."

"The same arrangement as before, please. Ring me up here when—"

"Excuse my interrupting. It's just on seven. The telephone to Ouistreham closes down at seven. . . . Unless you go to the mayor's place."

"Why?"

"He has a private line to Caen, and it's on all night."

"Send one of your men to the Exchange and tell him to listen in if anyone calls the mayor. Have you a car?"

"A runabout of sorts."

"Send someone in it to let me know if there's a call. The *Sailors' Rest* will find me, as before."

As he re-entered the public room, Delcourt ventured to ask:

"Are you on the track of the murderer?"

"Haven't an idea!"

The men in the café simply couldn't make out what had come over Maigret! He had seemed quite a good sort, a proper mixer. Now he was stand-offish, snapped a fellow's head off! He left the place without having vouchsafed a scrap of information.

Buttoning up his overcoat, he plunged again into the storm. As he crossed the bridge he felt it vibrating with the fury of the gale.

He walked to Joris's cottage and put his eye to the key-hole. There was a light in the kitchen. Behind the glass-panelled door someone was moving to and fro between the table and the range.

He rang. Julie stopped moving, put down the plate she was carrying, opened the kitchen door, and walked up the hall.

"Who is it?" she asked nervously.

"Inspector Maigret."

She unbolted the door and stood aside to let him pass. Her eyes were still red; she cast frightened glances round her.

"I'm so glad you've come. I can't bear being alone in this house, it gives me the creeps."

He went into the kitchen. It was spick-and-span as usual. On the white oilcloth covering the table were only bread and butter and a mug. A sickly-sweet smell came from a saucepan boiling on the fire.

"Hot chocolate?" He sounded surprised.

"Yes. I can't bring myself to cook a proper meal now I'm all alone."

"Carry on with your dinner," Maigret said. "Don't mind me!"

After some demur she complied, filled her mug, and began dipping thick slabs of bread and butter in the chocolate. As she munched, she gazed dully in front of her.

"Hasn't your brother been to see you yet?"

"No. I can't make it out. I went down to the harbor just now, hoping to see him. When they're off duty the sailors usually hang about the harbor and—"

"Did you know your brother was a bosom friend of the mayor's?"

She stared at him, open-eyed.

"What on earth do you mean?"

"At this moment they're playing draughts together."

Her first idea was that Maigret was pulling her leg. Then a frightened look settled on her face.

"I can't make head or tail of it."

"Why?"

"Well, the mayor isn't like that with folk like us. He keeps his distance. And anyhow, I know he don't like

Louis. He's always making trouble for him. Why, he even tried to prevent him living here."

"How about Captain Joris?"

"I don't follow."

"Was Monsieur Grandmaison on friendly terms with the Captain?"

"Just like he was with everybody else. Passed him the time o' day when they met in the street. Cracked a joke with him. Sometimes, as I told you, he took my gentleman out shooting. But only not to be alone."

"Has the lawyer written to you yet?"

"Yes. I'm the Captain's residuary legatee, he wrote; I don't know what it means. Does it mean I get the house?"

"Yes, and three hundred thousands francs as well."

She showed no interest, but went on eating. Presently she said:

"No, it don't make sense. I can't believe it. I'm certain the Captain never had that much money in all his life."

"Where did he sit? Did he dine in the kitchen?"

"Where you are, in that wicker chair."

"Did you eat together?"

"Yes. Only, of course, I got up to see to the cooking and bring the plates. He used to read the newspaper at dinner. Now and then he'd read a bit out loud."

Maigret was in no mood for sentiment. Yet somehow the restfulness of the atmosphere was having an effect on him. The clock seemed to tick more languidly than clocks elsewhere. A little blob of light swayed to and fro on the wall in front of him—reflected from the bright brass pendulum. The air was heavy with the cloying fumes of chocolate. The wicker chair emitted homely creaks as he shifted his legs, the same sounds as it must have made when Joris sat in it.

Being alone in the house made Julie nervous. Yet she

seemed reluctant to go elsewhere. Something, he guessed, kept her here, in these familiar surroundings.

She rose, went to the door. He kept his eyes on her. It was to let in the white cat. It went straight to a saucer of milk in front of the fire.

"Poor pussy! Her master was very fond of her. After dinner she always jumped on his knee and stayed there till he went to bed."

So profound was the calm as to seem almost ominous. A warm, enervating languor.

"Are you quite sure you've nothing more to tell me, Julie?"

She looked up and gazed at him in a puzzled way.

"I rather think," Maigret went on, "that I'm on the point of finding out the truth. A word from you might help enormously. That's why I ask if you have nothing more to tell me."

"But I've told you everything I know."

"Nothing more about Captain Joris?"

"Nothing."

"About your brother?"

"Nothing, I assure you."

"About someone else who came here, a stranger?"

"I don't know what you mean."

She went on eating the sugary mixture in the mug, the mere sight of which turned Maigret's stomach.

"In that case I'll be off."

She was obviously vexed at the prospect of being left alone again. A question rose to her lips.

"Please, about the funeral. . . . I suppose they can't keep waiting much longer. A corpse . . ."

"He's on ice," Maigret muttered uncomfortably.

Julie shuddered. . . .

+

"Are you there, Lucas?"

It was pitch-dark. The roar of wind and waves drowned all other sounds. At the lock men were waiting, each at his post, for a steamer from Glasgow that had missed the fairway and could be heard whistling down by the jetties.

"I'm here."

"What are they up to?"

"Eating—lucky devils! Shrimps, clams, an omelette, something that looks like cold veal."

"At the same table?"

"Yes. Louis still has his elbows on it."

"Talking?"

"Hardly at all. I can just see their lips move now and then, but they don't seem to have much to say."

"Drinking?"

"Louis, anyhow, is putting it down all right! There's two bottles of wine on the table—vintage stuff by the look of it—and the mayor keeps on filling up Louis's glass."

"Trying to make him drunk, eh?"

"Looks like it. I say, you should see the maid's face! Scared stiff she is! Every time she has to pass behind the big chap she gives him a wide berth."

"Any more telephone calls?"

"No. Ah, there's Louis blowing his nose with his napkin. He's getting a cigar. He's holding the box out to the mayor. The mayor's shaking his head. Here's the maid again, handing round the cheese." Plaintively Lucas added: "If only I could sit down a bit! My feet are like ice. And I daren't make a movement for fear of falling off my perch!"

But Maigret'd been too often in similar situations himself to feel much compassion for his junior.

"Stop grousing! . . . But I'll go and fetch you some grub."

A hot dinner awaited him at the *Hôtel de l'Univers*. But he merely spread a slice of bread with *pâté* and wolfed it, standing. Then he made a sandwich for Lucas and put the half-empty bottle of red wine in his pocket.

"That's a shame!" sighed the hotel-keeper. "I've made a *bouillabaisse* specially for you, and you wouldn't get a better one in Marseilles itself!"

But the Inspector was adamant. . . . He went back to the wall, and asked for the *n*th time the usual question:

"What are they up to now?"

"The maid has cleared away. The mayor's leaning back in his chair, smoking one cigarette after another. Louis seems to be going to sleep. He still has a cigar in his mouth, but no smoke's coming from it."

"Has he had more drinks?"

"A wine-glassful of the bottle on the mantelpiece."

"The Armagnac," Maigret murmured.

"Hullo! A light's just gone on, on the floor above. The maid going to bed, most likely. The mayor's rising to his feet. He's . . ."

A sound of voices down by the *Sailors' Rest*. The hum of an engine. People talking.

"A hundred yards up? In the house?"

"No, on the road."

The car had started. Maigret walked towards it. He stopped it some way down the road, not to alarm the people in the house. Policemen in uniform were in the car.

"Any news?"

"Evreux reports that the man in the yellow car has been caught."

"Who is he?"

"There's trouble about that. He's threatening to report us to his ambassador. Says he's been wrongfully arrested."

"A foreigner, eh?"

"Yes, Norwegian. Evreux told us his name over the 'phone. Something like Martineau, it sounded. Identity papers all O.K. Our fellows there are in a stew, want orders what to do next."

"Tell them to bring him here, with the car. They've an officer who can drive it, I suppose. Go back to Caen now. Try to find out where Madame Grandmaison usually stays in Paris."

"We know that already. At the Lutetia in the Boulevard Raspail."

"Then ring up, please, and find out if she's arrived and what she's up to. Wait a bit! If she's come there, ask the Superintendent in my office to have her shadowed by an inspector. Got it?"

The car had to back three times to turn on the narrow road. When Maigret returned, he found Lucas scrambling down from his perch.

"What are you up to?"

"Nothing more to be seen."

"Have they left the room?"

"No, but the mayor came to the window just now and drew the curtains tight."

A hundred yards away they saw a line of lights gliding into the lock, the Glasgow steamer. In a lull of the wind they heard orders bawled in English. Then a sudden gust all but whisked the Inspector's bowler hat away.

The light on the upper floor went out abruptly; the whole house now was plunged in darkness.

8. *The Mayor's Inquiry*

MAIGRET stood in the middle of the road, his hands thrust in his pockets, his brows wrinkled.

"Worried?" asked Lucas, who knew the signs.

"We've got to get inside the darned place somehow," Maigret growled, after gloomily inspecting the dark façade, window by window.

All were shut fast. There was no way of getting in except by the door, to which Maigret now went. He cocked his head, listened. Then signed to Lucas to keep still. Both pressed their ears to the smooth oak panels.

There was no talking. But from the study came a sound of heavy footsteps, and a dull, persistent thudding. It seemed unlikely that a fight was going on. The thuds were much too regular. When two men are fighting in a room, one expects to hear scuffling, furniture banged about, blows being dealt sometimes in quick succession, sometimes spaced out.

This was more of a steady pounding—like a pile-driver at work. By listening intently they could even hear the panting of the man who was delivering the blows.

A grunt at every stroke, followed by a stifled groan.

Maigret's eyes met the sergeant's. He pointed to the lock. Lucas drew a bunch of skeleton-keys from his pocket.

"Not a sound," Maigret whispered.

Silence had fallen in the house. An ominous lull. No more thuds. No footsteps. Only a faint, almost inaudible sound of gasping, as of a man who is out of breath.

Lucas straightened up. The door was open. On the left

a ray of light came from the study door. Maigret shrugged his shoulders petulantly. He was exceeding his rights, and knew it. What made things worse was that the man whose house he had broken into was no less a personage than the local mayor, and no easy customer at the best of times. Still, it had to be done. . . .

From the hall he could still hear only one man's breathing. Nothing stirred. Lucas fingered his revolver. Maigret flung the door open.

Then he stopped dead, for once completely flabbergasted. Perhaps he'd expected to be confronted by another crime. Very different was the scene before him—different and baffling to a degree.

His lip split, chin and dressing-gown streaming with blood, his hair disheveled, Monsieur Grandmaison looked like a boxer who has just struggled to his feet after severe punishment. He could hardly stand. Propped against the mantelpiece, he was leaning so far back that it was a mystery how he kept his footing on the polished floor.

Two yards away stood Louis, looking more ruffianly than ever, blood on his still clenched fists—the mayor's blood!

It was Louis they had heard panting when they were in the hall. Out of breath, no doubt, after the hammering he had given his victim. The glasses on the table had been upset. His breath reeked of alcohol.

The two police officers were so taken aback, the others so exhausted, that some minutes passed before a word was spoken.

Then Monsieur Grandmaison dabbed his lips with a corner of his dressing-gown, made an effort to pull himself erect, and spluttered:

"What . . . what the devil . . . ?"

"I trust you will excuse me," said Maigret in his politest

tone, "for entering your house like this. I heard a noise. The door was open."

"That's a lie," the mayor rejoined. His self-assurance had come back.

"In any case, I'm glad we came in time to protect you from . . ." He glanced towards Louis, who did not seem in the least embarrassed.

On the contrary, a furtive grin twisted his lips; he kept his eyes fixed on the mayor.

"I don't need protection," said Monsieur Grandmaison.

"But this man's assaulted you. . . . Or hasn't he?"

Standing in front of the mirror, Monsieur Grandmaison was trying to set his clothes to rights. His inability to stanch the flow of blood seemed to exasperate him. The picture he presented at that moment was a curious mixture of strength and weakness, abjection and bravado.

A black eye, scars, and bruises. The pink-and-white cheeks were in a lamentable plight, and there were greenish glints in his eyes.

Still, it was amazing, the promptness with which he was recovering his self-possession—and so effectively that now, propped against the mantelpiece, he rounded on his rescuers.

"I suppose you broke into my house?"

"Excuse me. . . . We came here to protect you."

"That's another lie! You didn't know that I was in any danger. And, what's more, I was *not* in danger," he added emphatically.

Maigret took a long look at Louis's formidable bulk. Not in danger!

"Still, I trust you will allow me to eject our friend here from your house."

"Certainly not."

"He's assaulted you. And in a pretty brutal way."

"We had a discussion. No concern of yours."

"May I take it that when you fell downstairs this morning, you—shall we say?—came in contact somehow with this fellow's fist?"

Louis's face split in a prodigious grin. He was thoroughly enjoying the situation. While recovering his breath he had not missed the least detail of the scene, a scene that had filled him with obvious glee. He, anyhow, knew what lay behind it, could relish its humor to the full.

"I informed you, Monsieur Maigret, that I was conducting an inquiry on my own account. I haven't interfered with your investigations; kindly do the same for me. And don't be surprised if I lodge a complaint against you for breach of domicile."

He cut a figure at once tragic and comical. He was trying to stand on his dignity. Straightening himself up to his full height. And all the time his lip was bleeding, his face battered to a pulp, his dressing-gown blood-stained, bedraggled.

And Louis gave the impression of egging him on.

It was easy enough to picture what had been happening in the room during the last ten minutes—the ex-convict sledge-hammering his victim's face till his arm was tired.

"You must excuse me, sir," said Maigret, "if I don't leave at once. As you have the only telephone available at night in Ouistreham, I ventured to arrange for my calls to be made here."

Without replying, Monsieur Grandmaison rapped out: "Shut the door."

Then he picked up one of the cigars lying scattered on the mantelpiece and tried to light it. The effect of the tobacco on his wounded lip was evidently painful, for he flung the cigar away impatiently.

Maigret said: "Lucas, will you call Caen for me?"

His eyes roved from the mayor to Louis, and back to the mayor. He was trying to set his thoughts in order. At first sight of the two men in the room it was Monsieur Grandmaison who had seemed to be the under-dog; in a state of not only physical but moral inferiority. He had been thrashed and exposed to the public gaze under the most humiliating circumstances.

And yet he had "saved his face"—if not quite literally! Within a few minutes he had taken hold of himself. With such success that much of the prestige due to his social rank was coming to the fore again. He was almost calm; his expression supercilious.

Louis had, ostensibly, the easier rôle. The top-dog's. Not a wound, not a scratch to show. A moment ago there had been a look of almost childish exultation on his face. Now, however, he was visibly wilting; he didn't know what to do with himself, where to look.

Maigret was reflecting: If one of the two men's the moving spirit, which is it? Hard to tell. Sometimes one would say, the mayor. Sometimes, Louis.

"Hullo! Caen police station? Inspector Maigret asks me to say that he's spending the night at the mayor's house. No. 1, Ouistreham. Yes, ring him up here. Hullo? What, Lisieux already? Thanks. Yes, I'll tell him." He turned to Maigret. "The car's just left Lisieux. They'll be here in three-quarters of an hour."

"Did I hear you say . . . ?" the mayor began.

"That I'd be here all night? Yes. With your leave, naturally. You've twice referred to an inquiry you are making on your own account. That being so, I suggest we pool the information each of us has managed to collect so far." He was not ironical. He was fuming inwardly. Raging at the predicament in which he had involved himself.

Furious, above all, that he couldn't make head or tail of the turn of events.

He turned to Louis.

"Will you tell me why, when we entered the house, you were engaged in . . . in beating up the mayor?"

Louis did not reply, but shot a glance at the shipowner, as if to say: *You* answer that!

Monsieur Grandmaison said curtly:

"That's my business."

"Obviously. Everyone has the right to let himself be beaten up if it amuses him," snapped Maigret. He was now in a tearing rage. "Lucas, ring up the Lutetia Hotel."

The blow struck home. Monsieur Grandmaison opened his mouth to speak. His grip tightened on the marble chimneypiece.

Lucas was holding the receiver.

"Three minutes to wait? Right. Thank you, yes."

"Doesn't it strike you, Monsieur Grandmaison," Maigret said, "that this inquiry's taking a rather peculiar turn? . . . By the way, perhaps you could do me a service. I expect that, as a shipowner, you've a wide circle of acquaintances, including foreigners. Have you ever heard of a man called Martineau or some such name? He comes from Bergen or Trondhjem. A Norwegian, though the name sounds French."

Silence. Louis's eyes grew hard. Unconsciously, it seemed, he reached towards one of the glasses lying on the table, filled it, drank it off.

"So you don't know him? A pity. He's coming here. . . ."

Well, he had drawn blank again. That settled it. He knew now that both men had decided on their line of conduct. Not to answer. Not to betray the least emotion.

Monsieur Grandmaison had changed his tactics. Still

with his back to the mantelpiece, his calves toasted by the
fire, he was staring at the floor with studied indifference.
. . . A grotesque face with its loosely molded features,
now mottled black and red and blue, a trickle of blood
along the chin, a look of strong determination oddly
combined with panic—or distress.

Louis was sitting astride a chair. After some yawns he
seemed to be dozing off.

The telephone rang. Maigret snatched up the receiver.

"Lutetia Hotel? Don't cut me off. I want to speak to
Madame Grandmaison. Yes. She came this afternoon or
evening. Right, I'll hold the line."

"I presume," the mayor said in a rather wooden voice,
"you don't intend to drag my wife into the, to say the
least of it, peculiar proceedings you're indulging in just
now?"

Maigret took no notice. He remained standing with the
receiver to his ear, staring at the table-cloth.

"Hullo? Yes? Oh, she's gone out. Wait! Let's start
at the beginning. When did this lady arrive? Seven.
Thank you. With her car and chauffeur. She dined at the
hotel. After dinner someone rang her up and she went
out at once. Right. No, that's all, thanks."

No one showed the least emotion. Monsieur Grandmaison seemed calmer. Maigret put back the receiver,
picked it up again.

"Caen telephone exchange? Police here. Will you tell
me if someone rang up Paris from this number before the
call I've just put through? Yes? About a quarter of an
hour ago. For the Lutetia Hotel, wasn't it? Thank you."

Beads of perspiration glistened on his forehead. Slowly
he filled a pipe and tamped the tobacco with his forefinger. Then he went to the table and helped himself to a
drink.

"I suppose you realize, Inspector, that everything you're doing here is quite illegal? You broke into my house. You're staying in it without my leave. The steps you've just taken are calculated to alarm my family, and, finally, you're treating me like a criminal in the presence of a third party. For all this, I warn you, you'll be brought to book."

"You've said it!"

"Well, as I'm no longer master in my own house, I'll ask your permission now to go to bed."

"No." Maigret pricked up his ears. He had heard the sound of an approaching car.

"Go and open the front door, Lucas."

Unthinkingly he put a shovelful of coal on the fire. He turned round at the exact moment the new-comers entered.

There were two constables from Evreux, a handcuffed man between them.

"You can go back," he said to the constables. "No, go to the end of the road and wait for me there—all night, if necessary."

The mayor had not moved. Nor had the sailor. They gave an impression of complete indifference; whether authentic or assumed there was no telling. The handcuffed man was calm; a smile rose to his lips when he saw Monsieur Grandmaison's battered face.

He glanced round the group.

"Who is in charge here, please?"

Maigret made a deprecatory gesture, as if to say the constables had gone beyond their orders; took a small key from his pocket and unlocked the handcuffs.

"Thank you. I must say I was greatly surprised at—"

Maigret broke in angrily.

"At what? At being arrested? Were you really so surprised as that?"

"Well, I'm still waiting to learn what charge is brought against me."

"For one thing, the theft of a bicycle."

"Not theft. I borrowed it. The garage-keeper from whom I bought the car will confirm that. I told him to send back the bicycle to Ouistreham, with a small sum as compensation to its owner."

"Did you now? . . . By the way, you're not a Norwegian."

The man had not the accent nor the look of one. He was tall, sturdy, middle-aged. His well-cut clothes were a little soiled.

"Excuse me, I am. Not by birth certainly, but I've been naturalized."

"And you live at Bergen, I believe?"

"At Tromsö, in the Lofotens."

"Have you a business there?"

"I own a factory for treating the waste products of the cod-fishing industry."

"Cod-roes, for instance?"

"Yes, the roes and other waste products. We extract oil from the heads and livers. And we use the bones to make a fertilizer."

"Capital! Just what I wanted! . . . Now, will you tell me what you were doing at Ouistreham on the night of September the sixteenth?"

The man showed no signs of confusion; he gazed calmly round the room.

"I was not in Ouistreham."

"Where were you?"

"Where were *you*?" He picked himself up, smiled. "I mean, could you possibly say, off-hand, exactly what you were doing on a given day, at a given time, when more than a month's elapsed?"

"Were you in Norway?"

"I expect so."

"Know this?" Maigret handed the man a gold fountain-pen.

"Thanks," he said, slipping it into his pocket without the least sign of trepidation.

A good-looking man, about the same age and height as the mayor, but slimmer, wirier. Dark eyes glowing with vitality. A smile on the thin lips, a smile of complete self-assurance.

He answered the Inspector's questions calmly, good-humoredly.

"May I assume," he said, "that there's been some mis-understanding? I'd like to be getting on to Paris."

"That's another matter. . . . Where did you first meet 'Big Louis'?"

The Norwegian's eyes did not, as Maigret had expected, swerve towards the sailor.

"Big Louis?" he repeated with a puzzled air.

"You met Joris, I take it, when he was on one of his voyages north?"

"Sorry! I don't follow. . . ."

"Naturally! And if I ask you why, instead of going to a hotel, you spent the night on a water-logged dredger, you'll go on staring at me like a stuffed owl, eh?"

"Well, really . . . ! Put yourself in my place."

"Yet it's a fact you came to Ouistreham last night on the *Saint Michel*. It's a fact you landed at the entrance of the harbor in the ship's boat. You went to the dredger and spent the night on board. This afternoon you came and had a look at the house where we now are, then 'bor-rowed' a bike and rode to Caen. You bought a car there. Drove towards Paris. Were you going to meet Madame Grandmaison at the Lutetia? If so, there's no point in your starting off again. Unless I'm greatly mistaken, she'll turn up here tonight."

There was a pause. The mayor stood rigid as a figure carved in stone, his eyes so set as to appear quite lifeless. Louis was still astride his chair, yawning, scratching his head. Seated when all the others in the room were standing, he seemed to dissociate himself from the proceedings. Maigret turned to the Norwegian.

"Your name is Martineau?"

"Yes, Jean Martineau."

"Well, Monsieur Jean Martineau, just think it over. Perhaps you may find you've something to tell me, after all. It's heavy odds on one of the persons in this room being sent up for trial before many days are out, let me inform you."

"And let *me* inform *you* that not only have I nothing to say, but I must ask your leave to communicate with my consul and ask him to take action."

Mere bluff—or was it bluff? The mayor had made a similar threat. Only Louis refrained from protest, taking the situation philosophically—provided drinks were forthcoming now and then.

Outside it was blowing great guns; with the full tide the gale had reached its maximum intensity.

The look on Lucas's face spoke volumes. He was obviously thinking: "Here's a pretty kettle of fish! If we don't get at something soon, we're in for it!"

Maigret was stumping up and down the room, puffing furiously at his pipe.

"So neither of you knows anything about what happened to Captain Joris, about his death?"

They shook their heads. Maigret's gaze kept coming back to Martineau.

A sound of hurried footsteps. A volley of agitated

knocks on the front door. After a moment's hesitation Lucas went and opened it. Someone burst into the room. It was Julie. Flustered, out of breath.

"Inspector!" she panted. "My brother . . ."

She stopped short, stared aghast at Louis, who was slowly raising his huge bulk from the chair, his eyes intent on her.

"Yes?" Maigret prompted. "Your brother, you were saying. . . . What about him?"

"Nothing. I . . . I only . . ."

She tried to smile, then made a hasty movement of retreat. As she did so she blundered into Martineau, glanced at him and, without seeming to recognize him, murmured: "Sorry, sir."

The door had been left open. A gust of clammy wind swept through the room.

9. *A Conspiracy of Silence*

JULIE told her story in little, breathless phrases.

"I was alone in the house. I felt nervous. I went to bed with my clothes on. Someone started banging at the front door. It was Lannec. My brother's captain, you know."

"So the *Saint Michel*'s in."

"She was in the lock when I went by. Lannec wanted to see my brother at once. They're in a hurry to sail, it seems. I told him Louis hadn't put his nose inside the house. He started mumbling something. I couldn't quite make out what he meant, but it made me frightened. . . ."

Louis was staring morosely at the floor. Now he shrugged his shoulders, as much as to say: "Just like a woman to get panicky over nothing!"

"Why did you come here?" Maigret inquired.

"I asked Lannec if Louis was in danger. He said 'Yes,' and perhaps it was too late already. So I ran down to the harbor, and they told me you were here."

Maigret turned to Louis.

"So you're in danger, are you?"

Louis's only answer was a huge guffaw, more uncouth even than his usual laugh.

"What was Lannec worried about, then?"

"How the hell should I know?"

Maigret's eyes settled on the faces of those present, one by one. He murmured pensively, if with a touch of irritation: "So it comes to this. Not one of you knows anything. You're all in the same boat. The mayor here doesn't know Monsieur Martineau, and he hasn't a notion why this fel-

low Louis, who to all appearances is a crony of his, after
an excellent dinner and a game of draughts, should suddenly start knocking him about."

No one spoke.

"Stranger still! You, Mayor, let Louis treat you like
this as if it was the most natural thing in the world! You
don't resist. You refuse to lodge a complaint. You don't
even tell the man to clear out."

He turned to Louis.

"You, too, know nothing. You spend a night on the
dredger, but you don't know who's with you on board.
You're entertained here like a lord, and all the gratitude
you show is to bash in your host's face. And, of course,
you've never set eyes on Monsieur Martineau!"

Not an eyelid twitched. All stared obstinately at the
carpet.

"And you, Monsieur Martineau, you're just as bad!
Your mind's a perfect blank. I wonder, do you even know
how you came here from Norway? No, I thought not.
You prefer dossing on a dredger to sleeping at a hotel.
You steal a man's bicycle, buy a car to go to Paris. But you
know nothing. You've never met Monsieur Grandmaison
or Captain Joris. . . . And you, Julie, naturally you
know even less than the others."

He gazed despondently at Lucas. Lucas understood the
look. It was out of the question arresting all these people.
There were grounds for suspicion—unaccountable behavior,
lies, inconsistencies—against each. But nothing definite
with which to charge them.

Maigret glanced at the clock. Eleven. Knocking out his
pipe over the fireplace, he said in his grumpiest tone:

"I must ask all of you to remain at the disposal of jus-
tice; though you profess to know nothing, I shall certainly
have further questions to put to you. May I assume, Mon-

sieur Grandmaison, that you have no intention of leaving Ouistreham?"

"Certainly."

"Thank you. You, Monsieur Martineau, can take a room at the *Hôtel de l'Univers,* where I'm staying."

The Norwegian bowed assent.

"Lucas, take this gentleman to the *Univers.*"

He turned to Louis and Julie.

"You two, come along with me."

Julie had started from home without an overcoat. Seeing her shivering, her brother took off his jacket and forced her to put it round her shoulders.

The noise of the storm made conversation almost impossible. They walked with their heads lowered, battling against an icy wind that whistled in their ears and lashed their cheeks, making their eyelids smart like fire.

The *Sailors' Rest* was brightly lit. For the moment the lock was clear of traffic and the lock-keepers were flocking down for "a quick one"—in most cases a hot grog. All eyes turned to Maigret and his two companions, and followed them as they struggled across the bridge in the teeth of the gale.

"Is that the *Saint Michel?*" Maigret sounded puzzled.

A schooner was coming out of the lock, but she looked much bigger than the *Saint Michel* as he remembered her.

"Aye, they're in ballast," Louis grunted.

Meaning that the schooner had unloaded her cargo at Caen and was now traveling empty to pick up a cargo at some other port.

They had nearly reached Joris's cottage when a dim form loomed up in front. In the darkness it was impossible to make out the man's face till he was almost touching them. A rather shaky voice addressed Louis:

"Ah, there you are. Hurry up! Time to get under way."

Maigret's gaze rested for a moment on the little Breton skipper's face; then veered seawards. Great waves were crashing on the breakwaters with a thunderous, incessant roar, and the sky was a welter of storm-clouds.

The *Saint Michel*, which had come alongside the jetty, was almost invisible but for the tiny flicker of a lamp hung on the deckhouse.

"Going out, are you?" asked Maigret.

"Aye."

"Where to?"

"La Rochelle. For a cargo of wine."

"Can't you manage without Louis?"

"D'you think two men can handle a ship in weather like this?"

Julie was half frozen, stamping her feet, as she listened to this conversation. Her brother's eyes wandered from Maigret to the schooner, from which came faint creaks of tackle straining in the gale.

"Go back to your ship," said Maigret to the skipper, "and wait for me on board."

"But . . ."

"But what?"

"In two hours' time it'll be too late. Tide's on the ebb." A glint of apprehension showed in his eyes. He was obviously ill at ease; his gaze shifted from one face to the other. "I gotta earn my living," he added.

Louis and he were exchanging furtive glances. Maigret spotted at once what was in the wind. His intuition was just then keyed up to its highest pitch. The little skipper was conveying by his look: "The schooner's quite close. There's only one warp to cast off. Lay this interfering flattie out and we can make a getaway."

Louis hesitated, gazed mournfully at his sister, sighed, shook his head.

"Go to your ship and wait," Maigret repeated.

"But—"

The Inspector turned on his heel and beckoned the others to follow him to the cottage. . . .

It was the first time he had seen brother and sister together. There was a good fire burning in Captain Joris's kitchen. The flue of the range was wide open, and at times the roaring of the flames gave place to a sudden detonation, like a backblast.

"Let's have something to drink," the Inspector suggested to Julie, who went at once to the cupboard and produced a bottle of spirits and three gaily painted glasses.

Maigret was conscious of being *de trop*. Julie was yearning for a heart-to-heart talk with her brother. His expression as he watched her told of a very real affection, not unmixed with a certain mawkish sentimentality.

After handing the two men their glasses, Julie, like the good little housewife she was, remained standing and busied herself with the fire.

"To the memory of Captain Joris," said Maigret, raising his glass.

There was a long silence. As the Inspector had intended. It gave time for the restful atmosphere of the little kitchen to take effect on Louis and his sister. And gradually the steady ticking of the clock, the drone of the stove, acted like music on their jangled nerves. The blood came back to their cheeks, which had been numbed by the blasts outside; their eyes brightened. The pungent fumes of Calvados rose in the air.

"Captain Joris," Maigret repeated musingly. "Why, I'm sitting just where he used to sit: in his armchair. This comfortable old wicker chair, which creaks every time one moves. If he was alive, I suppose he'd be coming back from the lock just about now. And he'd ask you for a glass of something to warm him up—eh, Julie?"

She gazed at him wide-eyed, then looked away.

"He wouldn't go up to bed at once, would he? He'd take off his boots. And you, Julie, would bring him his slippers. He'd say: 'A dirty night. And the *Saint Michel*'s gone out into the storm. Poor chaps, God protect them!'"

"How did you know?"

"What?"

"That he used to say 'God protect them!' when he'd seen a ship off on a night like this?"

She was greatly moved. She gazed at Maigret with a hint of gratitude in her eyes. Unlike Louis, who had a surly look.

"He'll never say it again. A shame, isn't it? He was happy. He'd a nice house, and lots of the flowers he was so fond of in his garden. Everyone liked him, so I'm told. And then—there was someone who put an end to all that, brutally—with a pinch of white powder in a tumbler."

Julie's features were quivering with the effort she was making to keep back her tears.

"A pinch of poison . . . and all was over. And the person who did it will, perhaps, lead a happy life, because nobody knows who that person is. Though I'm pretty sure he was amongst us an hour ago."

"Stop!" Julie implored, wringing her hands. The tears were flowing freely now.

But the Inspector knew where he was getting. He went on in a low voice, lingering on each word. There was very little play-acting in it; he was genuinely affected by the emotional atmosphere of the little room. A picture of the short, sturdy harbor-master was hovering before his eyes as he conjured up the past.

"Now he's dead and gone, he has only one friend left.

Myself! Fighting a lone hand to discover the truth and prevent the murderer from getting off scot free." Julie had broken down completely; she was sobbing violently as he went on. "But all the people who know anything about poor Joris's death refuse to speak. And lie so persistently that one can't help suspecting that every one of them has something to hide, that they're all accomplices."

"That's not true!" Julie burst out.

Louis was looking more and more uncomfortable. He filled up his glass, and the Inspector's as well.

"Louis, to begin with, keeps mum."

Through her tears Julie gazed anxiously at her brother, struck by the truth of the remark.

"He knows something. I believe he knows a great deal. Is he afraid of the murderer? Has he something on his conscience?"

"Louis!" Julie cried reproachfully.

But Louis looked away; his eyes hardened.

"Tell him it's not true, Louis. Please!"

"Dunno what the Inspector's gettin' at," Louis muttered. But he was so flustered that he rose from his seat.

"Louis is the biggest liar of the lot. He pretends not to know that Norwegian; and I'm certain he knows him. He pretends to have no dealings with the mayor, and I find him in the mayor's house, giving him a hiding."

The ghost of a smile flickered on the ex-convict's lips. But Julie was not appeased.

"Is that true, Louis?" He made no reply; she seized his arm. "Why don't you speak out? I *know* you haven't done anything wrong."

He shook his arm free. All the same, he seemed impressed. Was his resistance breaking down? Without giving him time to collect himself, Maigret went on:

"Yes, and very likely all that's needed to break this

tissue of lies is just a grain of truth, a tiny scrap of information."

No. For all his sister's entreating look, Louis merely gave his shoulders a great heave, like a giant shaking off the toils of pygmies, and growled:

"I don't know nothing."

"Why won't you speak?" Julie's tone was severe; her suspicion was aroused at last.

"I don't know nothing."

"The Inspector says . . ."

"Nothing, I tell you."

"Listen, Louis. I've always trusted you. You know that. And I've stood up for you, even to Captain Joris." An unlucky remark. She blushed, and made haste to change the subject. "Do please tell the Inspector all you know. I'm sick and tired of . . . of everything. And I won't stay in this house any longer, all by myself."

"Stop, Julie!" Louis murmured. "That's enough."

"What do you want him to tell you, Inspector?"

"Two things. Who Martineau is. And why the mayor lets himself be knocked about."

"Do you hear, Louis? It's nothing so very terrible."

"I don't know nothing."

Her anger rose.

"Louis, take care! I'll end by believing . . ."

The fire droned on monotonously, the clock ticked languidly, trailing glints of lamplight on its swaying pendulum. . . . And Louis looked absurdly out of place, with his huge bulk, his crooked head and shoulder—like some cave-man who had blundered into a trim and tidy cottage kitchen. He didn't seem to know what to do with his clumsy limbs, where to rest his shifty gaze.

"You *must* speak, Louis."

"I got nothing to say." His hand moved towards the bottle. She snatched it away.

"No. You've drunk quite enough already."

Her nerves were frayed to breaking-point. She dimly realized a crucial moment had come; hoped against hope the word would now be spoken that would clear up everything.

"Louis, this man—the Norwegian . . . Isn't he the gentleman that just bought the *Saint Michel* and said he was going to give you a job as skipper?"

An emphatic "No!"

"Then—who is he? He's never been seen in these parts before. And we don't have strangers coming here in winter."

"Dunno."

But she wouldn't give in, and her woman's wit suggested a new line of attack.

"The mayor's always been down on you. Is it true you had dinner with him this evening?"

"It's true."

She was trembling with impatience.

"But . . . For heaven's sake, Louis, tell me what it means. You *must*. Or I'll begin to think that . . ," Her voice broke. She was at the end of her tether. She stared helplessly at the old familiar things: the armchair, the range, the wall-clock, a glass jar painted with gaudy flowers.

"You were fond of the Captain. I know it. You've told me so heaps of times, and if you had a row with him it was because . . ." She realized this wanted clearing up. "I must explain, sir. I wouldn't like you to have wrong ideas. My brother really liked Captain Joris. And the Captain liked him too. Only they had—well, it wasn't exactly a row. Louis, you see, goes sort of crazy when he has money in his pocket. He just flings it away regardless. The Captain knew he used to come to me for help when he'd spent it all. So one day he gave him a good dressing-down about it. That's all. And that's why, later on, he forbade him to come to this house. To prevent him cadging money from me. But he always said that Louis was a decent fellow at bottom, only he was weak."

"And Louis," Maigret said deliberately, "may have known that, if Joris died, you'd inherit three hundred thousand francs."

It happened so quickly that the Inspector nearly got the worst of it. Julie screamed. Louis fell furiously upon Maigret, belabored him with his fists, then made a grab at his throat.

Just in time the Inspector's arm shot up, seized the man's wrist, and slowly but surely twisted it behind his back.

"Hands off!"

Julie had backed to the wall, covering her eyes with her arm, whimpering with terror. "Stop, Louis! Stop!"

Maigret released the man's arm.

"Now, Louis," he said peremptorily. "Out with it!"

"I've nothing to say."

"I've a good mind to arrest you."

"Please yourself."

"Inspector, sir," Julie wailed. "Please don't do that. Oh, Louis, I beg you, for heaven's sake, speak out."

The two men were standing by the door. Louis swung round. His cheeks were blazing red, his eyes glowing, his lips twisted in a curious grimace. He stretched out his arm towards his sister's shoulder in a sudden gesture of affection.

"Julie dear, I swear to you . . ."

"Don't touch me!"

He hesitated, took a step towards the hall, turned round again.

"Listen, Julie!"

"No. Go away!"

He walked slowly down the hall, behind Maigret; stopped at the door, thought for a moment of turning back —but gave it up. The door closed behind them. It opened again when they had taken only a few steps through the rain-swept darkness. They saw Julie's form outlined against the light; heard her call "Louis!"

Too late. Side by side the two men trudged towards the night-bound harbor. Within a few seconds the rain-squall had drenched them to the skin. From a pool of shadows a voice barked:

"That you, Louis?"

Lannec, on the *Saint Michel*, had heard their footsteps. His head bobbed up through the hatchway. Evidently he knew that Louis was not alone, for he went on in Low Breton:

"Jump on the fo'c'sle and we'll be off."

Maigret had understood. The night was so black that he could not see where the schooner's deck began and the quayside ended. His companion showed as a dark vacillating mass, his shoulders glistening under the downpour. He waited.

10. *On Board the* Saint Michel

LOUIS glanced towards the outer darkness of the sea; then, furtively, at Maigret. At last, shrugging his shoulders, he grunted to the Inspector:

"Coming on board?"

Maigret noticed that Lannec had something in his hand that looked like a rope's end. Watching him from the corner of an eye, he saw him pass it once round a bollard and bring it back on board. Which meant that the *Saint Michel* was made fast in such a way that he could cast off at a moment's notice without anyone's going ashore.

Maigret said nothing. He knew that he was playing a lone hand. Julie was a good three hundred yards away; he pictured her still sobbing in the kitchen. Besides her there was no one nearer than the people in the *Sailors' Rest*, half asleep by now in its comfortable warmth.

He stepped upon the bulwarks, then jumped down on to the deck. Despite the breakwaters, the sea was running high in the outer harbor and the *Saint Michel* pitching heavily.

The deck was in darkness but for some broken gleams of light from streaming spars. A dim form showed on the fo'c'sle: the captain, staring dumbfounded at the intruder. He wore rubber thigh-boots, an oilskin, a sou'wester. He was still holding the hawser.

All seemed waiting for something to happen. None was disposed to make the first move. Maigret could feel their eyes intent on him, and realized what a queer bird he must seem to them in his overcoat with a velvet collar, and the bowler he was grasping firmly to prevent its being blown away.

"You can't sail tonight," he said.

No protest. But a furtive exchange of glances between the skipper and Louis, meaning: "We'll sail all the same, eh?" and "Better not."

The gusts were so violent that it was almost impossible to remain on deck. Taking the lead again, Maigret walked to the hatchway, whose whereabouts he remembered.

"We'll have a talk. Tell the other man to join us."

He preferred to leave no one on deck. The four men clambered down the steep-pitched ladder. Oilskins and gum-boots were discarded. The lamp was lit. On the table lay a greasy chart, criss-crossed with pencil-marks. Beside it some empty glasses.

Lannec put two lumps of coal into the little stove. Then he gazed obliquely at his visitor, doubtful whether to propose a drink. The third man, Célestin, retreated to a corner, feeling ill at ease; it didn't seem natural his being asked down into the cabin.

The attitude of all three men made one thing perfectly clear: none of them was willing to speak out, because none of them knew exactly how things stood. The skipper kept shooting questioning glances at Louis, who gloomed back at him helplessly.

It looked as if a long preliminary explanation would be needed to start the ball rolling.

Lannec cleared his throat noisily and growled:

"Have you thought it over?"

Maigret, seated on a wooden bench, his elbows on the table, was fingering an empty tumbler. The glass was so thick as to be almost opaque.

Louis, who was standing, had to stoop to avoid touching

the roof with his head. To keep himself in countenance, Lannec was fumbling with something in the cupboard.

"Thought what over?" Maigret inquired.

"I don't know what your powers are. But I do know this: that I take my orders only from the shipping authorities. It's for them to decide whether a ship leaves port or not."

"Well?"

"You're stopping me from leaving Ouistreham. I've cargo to take on at La Rochelle, and there's a penalty for every day I'm overdue."

An unpromising beginning, this; on a grave, semi-official note. But Maigret was getting used to this sort of thing. Hadn't the mayor taken much the same line? And Martineau, with his allusions to his consul.

He took a deep breath, then darted a quick glance at the three men. His eyes were twinkling.

"Don't try to come the sea-lawyer over me!" he said in Breton. "What about a drink?"

It might have fallen flat. The old sailor merely gaped at Maigret. Louis, however, visibly unstiffened. Lannec, still on his guard, asked:

"Are you a Breton?"

"Not quite. My home town's on the Loire. But I went to school at Nantes."

Disdainful looks. The scorn of the true-born, seafaring Breton for the inlander, and especially for the half-caste Bretons of the Nantes district.

"Got any more of the Hollands we had the other day?"

Lannec fetched the bottle and filled the glasses slowly, glad to have something to occupy him. He was still uncertain what line to take. Bluff and burly, his bowler well back on his head, puffing at his pipe, Maigret seemed to have made himself quite at home in the little cabin.

"Why not sit down, Louis?"

Louis complied. The ice wasn't broke yet, but now the men's constraint came from a different cause: from not being able to respond to Maigret's geniality in kind. The trouble was, they had to be on their guard.

"Here's luck, my lads! And you can't deny that by stopping you from sailing on a filthy night like this I'm doing you a good turn."

"If it wasn't for the gut. . . ." Lannec took a deep swig of his gin. "Once we're clear of that it's all right. But the river runs at the hell of a pace, and what with the current and the sand-banks, it takes some doing, getting through the gut. Every year there's some ships run aground there."

"The *Saint Michel*'s never been in trouble, eh?"

Lannec hastily touched wood. From his corner Célestin growled an angry protest.

"Not she! She's a daisy; there ain't another like her. Listen to this! Last year she ran aground in a thick fog on the English coast. A rocky shore and a big sea running. Any other ship'd have broken up. Well, when the tide rose she just floated off. Hadn't even to go into dry dock."

So long as he kept to that topic, Maigret knew the going would be good. But he was not out to listen to sea-talk all night. . . . Water was coming in from the deck, trickling down the ladder; steam rising from the men's rain-soaked clothing. And, not to put too fine a point on it, the heaving of the ship, which now and again bumped heavily against the piles, was telling on the Inspector's innards.

"She'll make a good private yacht," he remarked with seeming casualness.

Lannec gave a slight start.

"Aye, she *could* be made into a fine yacht," he amended. "Only the deck to change. And cut down her canvas a bit, especially up aloft."

"Has the Norwegian clinched the deal?"

Lannec shot a quick glance at Louis. Louis sighed. The two men would have given much for a few seconds' private talk together. What had Louis divulged? The skipper had no idea what line to take.

Louis had a hang-dog air. He knew what was coming. In a proper jam they were! And no way of passing the word to Lannec. Trouble brewing, whatever way one looked at it. The best thing was to drink. He poured himself out a glass of Hollands, swallowed it at a gulp and faced up to the Inspector. But there was little hostility in his manner; merely resignation.

"What Norwegian?"

"Well, the Norwegian who isn't a real Norwegian. That chap Martineau. It can't have been at Tromsö that he saw the *Saint Michel*, as she's never gone so far north."

"Not but what she couldn't," the skipper said. "She's good for a voyage to Archangel any day o' the year."

"When's he taking delivery?"

From his corner the old sailor emitted a derisive grunt. The derision was not aimed at Maigret, but at the ship's company at large—himself included. Lannec found nothing better than a lame rejoinder:

"Don't know what you're talking about."

Maigret's response was a playful dig in the ribs.

"Tell that to the marines! Now look here, my lads! Stop pulling those long faces at me, like mourners at a funeral—or the damned pig-headed Bretons you are. Martineau's said he'll buy the schooner. Has he put through the deal or not?" He had an inspiration. "Just show me the crew-list."

One up to him! He read it in their faces.

"Don't know where I've stowed it."

"Lannec, I told you not to play the fool. Hand over that document, damn your eyes!"

He had struck the right note—a mixture of truculence and cordiality. The skipper went to the cupboard, fished out a moldy attaché-case. It contained official documents and business letters headed with the titles of shipbrokers' firms.

There was also a big brand-new yellow folder in which had been inserted some imposing-looking foolscap sheets, the crew-list. Dated September 11—i.e. five days previous to the disappearance of Captain Joris.

Schooner Saint Michel. 270 *Tons Gross. Licensed for Coastal Navigation. Owner: Louis Legrand, Port-en-Bessin. Master: Yves Lannec. Deck-hand: Célestin Grollet.*

Louis poured himself out another glass. Lannec looked down, embarrassed.

"Aha! So you're the owner of this ship at present, Louis?"

No answer. In the corner Célestin had started munching a quid of black tobacco.

"Listen to me, my lads. It's no use beating about the bush. I can see through a brick wall as well as the next man. Though I mayn't know much about the sea, I do know this—that Louis hasn't a penny to his name. Well, a ship like this costs at least a hundred and fifty thousand francs."

"More," Lannec cut in. "Wouldn't 'a' sold her at that price."

"Right! Say, two hundred thousand. It's clear that Louis

has bought her for someone else. Let's say, for Martineau.
For some reason or other, Martineau doesn't want it
known he owns the schooner. . . . Here's luck!"

Célestin shook his shoulders as if the whole proceedings
disgusted him profoundly.

"Was Martineau at Fécamp on the eleventh of September, when the sale took place?"

Sour looks all round. Louis picked up the quid of tobacco which was lying on the table and took a bite, while
Célestin spattered the cabin floor with clots of brownish
spittle.

There was a break in the conversation. The lamp had
begun to smoke, the oil had run out, and the can was on
deck. Lannec came back soaked through. For a minute
or two the cabin was in darkness. When the lamp was lit
again everyone was in the same place as before.

"Martineau was there, I'm positive of that. The ship
was bought in Louis's name, but it was agreed that Lannec
stayed with her; perhaps for good, perhaps for a short
time."

"Only for a while."

"Exactly. I'd guessed as much. Long enough to use the
Saint Michel for a rather queer sort of cruise." Lannec rose
from his seat, so flustered that he bit through his cigarette.
"You came to Ouistreham," Maigret went on. "On the
night of the sixteenth the *Saint Michel* was moored in the
outer harbor, ready to go to sea. Where was Martineau?"
The skipper sat down again, despondent but determined
not to speak. "On the morning of the sixteenth the *Saint
Michel* sailed. Who was her passenger? Was Martineau
still on board? Was Joris with you?"

Maigret did not put his questions in the tone of an
examining magistrate; not even in that of a police officer.
His manner was completely cordial, there was a humorous

twinkle in his eye. He might have been playing a guessing game at a family party.

"You went to England. Then you set a course for Holland. Was it there that Martineau and Joris left the ship? For they certainly went farther north. To Norway, I've every reason to believe."

Louis emitted a sort of growl.

"What did you say?"

"That you'll never find out. . . ."

"Was Joris already wounded when he came on board? Or was he wounded during the voyage, or later on, in Norway?" He knew better than to expect an answer, and went on at once: "The three of you carried on with your coasting business as before. But you kept to the north coast. You were awaiting a letter or telegram fixing a meeting-place. Last week you were in Fécamp, the port where Martineau first got in touch with you. There Louis learnt that Captain Joris had been found in Paris, in a queer state, and was being brought back to Ouistreham. Louis came here by train. Found no one in the Captain's house. Left a note for his sister and went back to Fécamp."

Maigret heaved a sigh, paused to relight his pipe.

"Well, we're getting near the end of the story. Martineau was at Fécamp and you brought him here with you. But you dropped him at the entrance of the harbor. Which proves he didn't want to be seen. Louis and he arranged to meet on the dredger. . . . Here's the best!"

He helped himself and drained his glass. The three men watched him apathetically.

"When all's said and done, the only thing I'd like to know is what Louis was up to when he went to see the mayor—while Martineau was driving towards Paris. Queer doings anyhow—bashing in the face of a man who has the reputation of being a bit high hat, especially in his dealings with common folk like you and me."

Louis couldn't repress a grin of satisfaction at this reminder of his prowess.

"So that's how it stands, my lads. Try and ram it into those thick heads of yours that sooner or later we'll get to the bottom of it all. Don't you think it would be better to come out with it right away?"

Maigret tapped his pipe out against his heel to empty it; then started refilling it. Célestin was fast asleep. Snoring, his mouth wide open. Louis, his head cocked on one side, was staring at the dirty floor. Lannec was vainly trying to catch his eye, hoping to be given a lead. At last he muttered:

"We've nothing to tell you."

A crash on the deck. As if some heavy object had dropped on it. Maigret started. Louis put his head and shoulders through the hatchway, his legs remaining visible along the ladder. Had he gone right up on deck, the Inspector would have followed.

For at most half a minute Louis remained thus. There was no sound except the patter of the rain on the deck, the creak of tackle. Then he climbed down again, water streaming down his cheeks, his wet hair plastered on his forehead. He vouchsafed no explanation.

"What was it?"

"A block."

"How did it make that noise?"

"Fetched up against the bulwarks."

The skipper replenished the stove. Did he believe Louis's explanation? In any case, Louis made no response to his looks of anxious inquiry. He shook Célestin's shoulder.

"Go and bend on the mizzen-sheet."

The seaman rubbed his eyes. The order had to be repeated twice before it soaked into his sleep-fuddled brain. Then he got into his oilskin and sou'wester and dragged himself up the ladder, furious at being bundled out of the warm cabin into the wind and rain.

They could hear his wooden clogs clattering on the deck overhead as he moved to and fro. Louis helped himself to a drink, his sixth or seventh; but drink apparently took no effect on him. No change had come over the coarse, rather bloated face, with the large shallow eyes and the look of a born drifter, one of life's misfits.

"Well, what about it, Louis?"

"About what?"

"Don't play the fool! You know what I mean. Don't you realize you're up against it? For one thing, you've your past against you. You've served a term. No getting away from that. Then there's the purchase of this ship, when you hadn't a sou. Then there's the fact that Joris showed you the door because you were always sponging on Julie. And the fact that the *Saint Michel* was here on the night he was kidnapped. You were here, too, on the day he was poisoned. And your sister's inherited three hundred thousand francs from him."

The words might have fallen on deaf ears. Louis's eyes were perfectly expressionless. Vacant as a doll's eyes; staring at the wall in front of him.

"What's he up to on deck?" Lannec sounded worried. He stared at the half-open hatch through which water was streaming in, forming a puddle on the floor.

Maigret had not drunk much. Enough, however, to bring the blood to his head, especially in this stuffy atmosphere. Enough, too, vaguely to stimulate his imagination.

He fell to picturing the life of these three men, whom

he now knew fairly well, in this small universe of theirs, the *Saint Michel*.

Always a bottle and some dirty glasses on the table. One man sprawling in his bunk, fully dressed most of the time. The others on deck, the tramp of clogs or sea-boots resounding overhead. And always that steady, muffled throbbing of the sea. The binnacle with its little light. Another lamp swaying on the mizzen-mast.

He pictured them peering into the darkness, watching for the far-off gleam of a lighthouse. Then on the wharves, unloading cargo. Two or three days of leisure, spent in pubs, all alike in every port. . . .

Maigret pricked up his ears. There were sounds he couldn't account for overhead. . . . The alarm-clock hung on the wall said three o'clock. Louis looked as if he too were drowsing off. The bottle was almost empty.

Yawning, Lannec fumbled in his pocket for cigarettes. . . .

Maigret fell to thinking of the night when Joris disappeared. Might they not have spent it in this stuffy, overheated cabin, noisome with the smells of coal-tar and unkempt humanity? And perhaps he too had drunk with them, struggled to fight down sleep.

There was no mistaking now the sounds on deck; they were men's voices. But, blurred by the gale, they reached the cabin as an unintelligible murmur.

Maigret rose, frowning. Lannec, he saw, was filling his glass again; Louis's eyes were almost closed, his chin sunk on his chest.

Maigret took out his revolver and began to climb the ladder.

It was almost vertical, and the hatchway only just wide enough for a man's body to pass. The Inspector was bulkier than the average.

So he never had even a sporting chance. No sooner had his head emerged above the deck than a gag was slipped across his mouth and knotted tightly behind his head. Dirty work—by Célestin and another deck-hand, most likely.

Meanwhile someone wrenched his revolver from his right hand and tied his wrists together behind his back.

He lashed out backwards with his foot; hit something which felt like a face. But then a rope coiled round his legs.

"Heave away!" Louis's voice. Dull, phlegmatic as ever.

That was the hardest part. The Inspector was no light weight. From below they pushed him, while the men above hauled at his shoulders.

Rain was falling in torrents, the wind roaring up the canal with redoubled violence.

The masthead light had been put out, but Maigret thought he could distinguish the forms of four men. But the abrupt change from a warm lighted room to bitter cold and darkness had numbed his senses.

"One. Two. Three. Hoist!"

Like a sack of flour he was heaved up from the deck, swung across the bulwarks, and dumped on the slimy cobbles of the wharf.

Louis stepped on shore and tested the knots one by one. For a moment the Inspector glimpsed the ex-convict's face quite close to his. He had an impression that it had a bored, dejected look, as if he were engaged in a task that went against the grain.

"Tell my sister . . ." he began.

Tell her what? He didn't know himself. From the schooner came sounds of hurrying feet, creaking pulleys, flapping canvas, muttered orders. The jibs were unfurled. The mainsail crept slowly up its mast.

"Tell her, please, that I'll see her again one day. You, too, perhaps."

He jumped back on to the deck. Maigret was lying with his eyes towards the sea. A lantern on a halyard ran up to the masthead. A dark form moved beside the tiller.

"Cast off!"

Hauled in on board, the rope slipped off the bollard. The jibs flapped and the bow payed off. The schooner almost swung completely round, caught by the full force of the squall. Just in time a push at the tiller brought her up into the wind. For a while the ship seemed to hesitate, as if feeling for her course. Then suddenly, heeling over, she shot between the jetties.

A black mass in the darkness. A tiny glimmer of light on the deck and another high up on the mast, a lone star wandering in a stormy sky.

Maigret couldn't move. He lay helpless in a pool of water—on the edge of an abyss of darkness.

He was thinking: Probably they've finished off the bottle of Hollands by now. Dutch courage. The skipper's put a couple of lumps of coal on the fire. One man at the helm. The other two sprawling in their wet bunks.

There may have been one salty drop amongst the raindrops streaming down the Inspector's cheeks. What a come-down for a mighty man of valor, the most robust, intrepid representative of no mean Force, the *Police Judiciaire*, to spend an abject night, trussed up like a bale of piece-goods, on the cobbles of a little wharf!

Had it been possible for him to turn, he would have seen the small wooden porch of the *Sailors' Rest*, dark and deserted now.

11. *The Sand-Bank*

THE tide was ebbing fast. Maigret heard the surf breaking on the end of the breakwater; then, more faintly, receding down the sands.

With the ebb the wind fell, as usually happens. The shafts of rain lost their sting, and by the time the lowering clouds were graying with the dawn, the downpour of the night had changed to a thin, but still icier, drizzle.

Little by little, objects were emerging from the murk; slender black lines took form across the grayness—the slanted masts of fishing-smacks that were lying stranded on the mud-flats of the outer harbor.

Far away inland a cow mooed. A church-bell started ringing, with discreetly gentle chimes, for seven o'clock Low Mass.

But Maigret knew he would have to wait quite a while yet. The churchgoers wouldn't come this way; nor would the lock-keepers show up before high water. There was always the chance a fisherman might walk by; but, considering the weather, that hope, too, seemed pretty remote.

Shivering in his sodden clothes, Maigret pictured enviously all the beds of Ouistreham: stout oak beds straddled by fat eiderdowns, and people sleeping in them the sleep of the just, between soft warm blankets. With his mind's eye he saw them blinking at the gray glimmer of dawn upon the panes, then settling down for another forty winks before venturing their bare feet on the cold floor.

Was Sergeant Lucas, too, in bed? Not likely, for in that case all that had happened was quite inexplicable.

Maigret's theory of it was this. Martineau had somehow or other managed to put Lucas out of action. Quite possibly by trussing him up too. Then he had come to the *Saint Michel*. Hearing the Inspector's voice, he had hung about till somebody showed up. Probably when Louis had put his head through the hatchway he'd whispered instructions to him, or given him a note.

The rest was child's-play. A noise on deck. Célestin sent up to see. A conversation between the two men to lure Maigret up the ladder. When he was half-way up, the men on deck had gagged him while those below secured his legs.

By now the schooner must be outside territorial waters, which end three miles from the coast. Except in the unlikely event of her putting in at another French port, Maigret could take no steps to intercept her.

He kept quite still. He had noticed that each time he moved it let more water in beneath his overcoat.

His ear was resting on the ground and he could account for all the sounds that came to it; for instance, the clank of the pump in Joris's yard.

So Julie was up. She had gone out in her clogs to fetch the water for her morning wash. But she wasn't likely to leave the premises. It was still rather dark; probably she'd lit the lamp in the kitchen.

Footsteps. Someone crossing the bridge. Walking slowly. The footsteps approached, along the edge of the jetty. Something—it sounded like a coil of rope—was thrown down into a row-boat alongside.

Probably a fisherman. With an effort Maigret heaved himself over, and saw the man, twenty yards away, about to climb down the iron ladder leading to the water. In spite of the gag, he managed to utter a weak cry.

The fisherman looked round, noticed the black mass lying on the ground, and eyed it suspiciously for some moments before coming up to investigate.

"Whatcher doing there?" he began. Then, vaguely remembering something he'd heard about the correct procedure when confronted by a crime, he drew back. "I guess I'd better go and fetch the police."

However, he removed the gag. After some talk the Inspector succeeded in persuading him—though he still had misgivings—to unfasten the ropes as well. The fisherman had some hard words for the "feller what made these here knots."

Up at the pub the waitress was opening the shutters. Though the gale had abated, the sea was still running high, but without the thunderous roar of the night that had just ended. A huge wave swept in from the open sea, rising on the sand-bank to a solid wall of water ten feet high, and broke with a prodigious crash that seemed to shake the earth.

The fisherman, a wizened old seadog with a bushy beard, still showed signs of compunction.

"Gotta inform the police, you know."

"But I told you just now that I'm a police officer myself, a sort of plain-clothes policeman."

"Aye, a plain-clothes policeman, so you says." He was still worried, doubtful what to do.

As he pondered, his gaze roved seawards, scanning the horizon. Suddenly it came to rest on a point to the right of the jetty. He turned and stared at Maigret with a look of consternation.

"What's up?"

The fisherman was too perturbed to answer, and Maigret

only understood when he too had swept his gaze round the horizon.

It was near low water, and the bay showed as a vast stretch of golden sand extending over a mile out, edged by a ribbon of foam.

To the right of the jetty, little more than half a mile away, a boat had run aground, half of her resting on the sand, the other half lashed by gigantic waves. Two masts, one with a square lantern. A Paimpol schooner, judging by her build. Beyond all doubt, the *Saint Michel*.

In that direction all was gray, the skyline indistinguishable from the sea. Against the grayness, a black slanting mass: the schooner's hull.

"Reckon they sailed too late after the full," remarked the fisherman.

"Does that happen often?"

"Aye, it's happened afore now. Weren't enough water at the gut. And the current from the Orne pushed 'em again the bank."

A veil of driven rain and spindrift lay across the sea, giving a strangely forlorn remoteness to the scene. Still, when one saw the schooner almost on dry land, it was difficult to believe that those on board had faced any real danger.

But when she had put out, the sea had still been breaking at the foot of the dunes. Ten ranks of mountainous waves between her and the sand-bar.

"Got to tell the harbor-master."

A trivial detail. Unthinkingly the man started off towards Joris's cottage. Then, muttering something, he swung round and walked in the opposite direction.

Meanwhile, however, the wreck had been observed by others, perhaps from the church porch. Captain Delcourt with three other men came bustling up. Delcourt still seemed half asleep. He shook hands absent-mindedly, failed to notice that Maigret looked like a drowned rat.

"I warned them not to do it."

"Ah, so they told you they were leaving last night."

"Well, when I saw that they had moored down here I guessed that they weren't going to wait for the next tide, and I advised the skipper to beware of the current."

Everyone moved down to the beach. It was heavy going. They had to wade through patches of water a foot deep; their boots sank into the wet sand.

"Are they in any danger?" Maigret asked.

"Oh, they're off the ship already. Or else they'd be on the look-out for us, and they'd have run up the distress signal." He suddenly looked worried. "Wait a bit, though! They hadn't got their boat with them. You remember? After that steamer brought it in, we kept it in the dock."

"Well?"

"It means they must have swum ashore. Or else . . ."

Delcourt was uneasy. There were several queer features about the wreck.

"What puzzles me," he said, "is why they didn't shore up the schooner, to prevent her heeling over. Unless she heeled over the moment she struck. It's devilish odd in any case!"

On a close-up view the *Saint Michel* was a dismal sight. Her keel was painted a livid green, her hull crusted with barnacles. The men who had come with Delcourt prowled round the schooner, looking for signs of injury. None was found.

"It's just an ordinary grounding."

"No damage done?"

"No. At next high water a tug will pull her off easily enough. Only I still don't understand . . ."

"What don't you understand?"

"Why they abandoned ship. It's not like them to get the wind up. And they know the schooner's stoutly built. You can see that for yourself. . . . Hi there, Jean-Baptiste! Go and fetch a ladder."

Even with the list, the deck was well above their heads.

"Don't need a ladder, sir."

A broken shroud was hanging over the side. The man swarmed up it, dangled a moment in mid-air, then swung himself on to the deck. Some minutes later he let down a ladder.

"Anyone on board?"

"Not a soul."

Some miles away along the coast Maigret could see the houses of Dives and factory smoke-stacks; and, farther on, less clearly, Cabourg, Houlgate, and the cliffs behind which lay Deauville and Trouville. "I suppose I'd better have a look on board," he murmured.

He scrambled up the ladder. Once on board, the slope of the deck made him feel quite dizzy, more squeamish than if the ship had been rolling heavily. Broken glass strewed the cabin floor. Cupboard doors stood open.

The harbor-master was in a quandary. The ship was not his. Dare he take the responsibility of sending to Trouville for a tug and having her refloated?

"If she stays here for another tide she'll be a total wreck," he muttered.

"In that case, do all that can be done to save her. You can say you acted on my instructions."

Meanwhile the eyes of the men on board had swung round towards the empty dunes; it almost looked as if they expected to see the crew of the *Saint Michel* there, watching their operations. Never had the sense of vague foreboding been so pronounced as it was now. . . .

On his way back to Ouistreham Maigret passed a steady

stream of men and children hurrying down to the beach. On the outskirts of the harbor Julie buttonholed him.

"Is it true? Have they been wrecked?"

"No. They only ran aground. There's no need to fear for a good swimmer like your brother."

"Where is he?"

A melancholy business; a jig-saw puzzle where the pieces didn't match. As Maigret was walking by his hotel the proprietor hailed him.

"Your two friends aren't down yet. Shall I wake them?"

"Don't bother. I'll go myself."

He went upstairs to Lucas's room. Lucas was lying on his bed tied up almost as tightly as Maigret had been.

"Let me explain . . ."

"No need. Come along!"

"Any fresh developments? . . . But you're soaked through. You look done in!"

Maigret went with him to the post-office, which was opposite the church, at the end of the village. Everyone who could get away was hurrying down to the beach; the others were standing on their doorsteps.

"So you'd no chance of resisting him?"

"No. We were going up to bed. He was behind me on the stairs. Suddenly he grabbed my legs. It all happened in a flash. I hadn't a chance of hitting back. . . . Have you seen him?"

Maigret created quite a sensation. He looked as if he'd been standing all night up to his neck in water. Impossible to write; the water trickled down his arms on to the paper.

"You write, Lucas. Wires to all police stations and mayors in the district. Dives, Cabourg, Houlgate. Places south, as well. Luc-sur-Mer, Lion, Coutances. Study the map. Even the smallest villages within ten miles from the sea.

"Descriptions of four men. Louis, Martineau, Captain Lannec, that old codger they call Célestin.

"After sending off the telegrams, ring up the nearest towns and villages; that'll save time."

He left Lucas busy writing out the wires, and crossed to a small pub facing the post-office. There he gulped down a hot grog while the village children flattened their noses against the panes, watching him.

All Ouistreham was humming with excitement. Everyone gazing, or walking, seawards. The wildest rumors were afloat.

On the road Maigret encountered his rescuer, the old fisherman.

"Look here, my man! I hope you haven't been telling . . ."

"I said as how I'd found you," the man replied indifferently.

The Inspector gave him twenty francs, and went to the hotel to change. He was feeling dithery, hot and cold all over. He had dark pouches under his eyes, a thick growth of bristles on his chin.

Yet, tired as he was, his brain was active. Even more so than usual. He managed to take note of all he saw, answer people and put questions to them, without once losing grip of the ordered sequence of his thoughts.

It was nearly nine when he returned to the post-office. Lucas was near the end of his telephone calls. The telegrams had already been despatched. All police stations reported that none of the persons wanted had been traced so far. Maigret turned to the telephone operator.

"Has Monsieur Grandmaison put through a call?"

"Yes, an hour ago. To Paris."

She gave him the number. He looked it up in the directory; it was a school, the *Collège Stanislas.*

"Does the mayor often call that number?"

"Fairly often. I think his son's there."

"Ah, yes, he has a son. The boy's about fifteen, isn't he?"

"I believe so. I've never seen him."

"Hasn't Monsieur Grandmaison rung up Caen?"

"No, but he had a call from there. From a member of his family, or his office staff; from his own house, anyhow."

The telegraph began clicking. A message for the harbor-master: *"Tug Athos arriving noon. Trouville Harbor Office."*

At last a telephone call from Caen police station. "Madame Grandmaison reached Caen at 4 A.M. Slept at her house in the Rue du Four. She's just left in her car for Ouistreham."

When Maigret, from the harbor, looked out to sea, the tide had gone out so far that the stranded schooner lay midway between the sea-line and the dunes. Captain Delcourt was scowling. Everyone was gazing anxiously at the horizon.

For there was no mistaking the signs. The wind had fallen with the ebb, but with the turn of the tide it would start blowing again, and harder than ever. The sullen gray sky and the color of the water, a livid green, were sure precursors of a gale.

"Has anyone seen the mayor?"

"His maid was here just now. He'd asked her to say he's ill and leaves everything to me."

Maigret trudged uphill to the major's house, his hands thrust in his overcoat pockets. He rang. Ten minutes passed before the door opened.

The maid began to say something. Brushing her aside,

he walked straight in. His manner was so determined that she dared not protest, and merely hurried ahead of him to the study door. There she announced in a loud voice:

"The Inspector's here, sir."

The bruises on the mayor's face showed up much more than on the previous night, being blue instead of red. A big coal fire was burning in the fireplace.

Monsieur Grandmaison's expression conveyed a firm resolve not to speak; indeed, wholly to ignore his visitor's presence. Maigret took a similar line. After depositing his coat beside his hat, which he had placed on a chair on entering, he planted himself squarely on the hearthrug, with his back to the fire and the air of a man whose only care is to get warm. He puffed vigorously at his pipe.

"Well, well"—he sounded as if he were talking to himself—"it's a relief to know the inquiry will be over by tonight."

The mayor made a slight movement, quickly repressed. He picked up a newspaper beside his chair and pretended to read it.

"I'm afraid, by the way, we may have to go to Caen, and you'll have to come with us."

"To Caen?" Monsieur Grandmaison looked up, puckering his brows.

"Yes. I really should have let you know sooner. It would have saved Madame Grandmaison the trouble of a needless journey here."

"I fail to see what my wife . . ."

". . . has to do with it," Maigret completed the remark. "So do I, for that matter!"

His pipe had gone out. He went to the desk, took a box of matches and lit it again.

"Anyhow, that's a mere detail," he said in a more casual tone, "as everything's to be cleared up quite soon. By the way, do you know who the present owner of the *Saint Michel* is? Louis, of all people! The nominal owner, anyhow. Probably he's only a man of straw and the real owner's a man called Martineau. . . . Wonder if they'll succeed in towing her off the sand-bank?"

The mayor was obviously trying to discern what lay behind these desultory remarks. But he refrained from speaking; especially from putting questions.

"Now you can see how it all hangs together. Louis bought the *Saint Michel* for Martineau five days before Joris disappeared. She's the only ship that left Port Ouistreham immediately after his disappearance, and she called in at British and Dutch ports before returning to France. Now, there are certainly coasting-boats of the same type plying between Holland and Norway. Before he went to Paris with his skull patched up, Captain Joris was taken to Norway."

The mayor was all attention now.

"That's not all. Martineau came back to Fécamp when the *Saint Michel* was there. Louis, who acts as his factotum, was here some hours before Joris's death. The *Saint Michel* followed up a little later, with Martineau on board. Last night he tried to make a getaway, along with the men I ordered to stay here at my disposal. With one exception —you."

Maigret paused, then added with a sigh:

"Two facts are still unexplained. Why Martineau returned and tried to go to Paris. And why you rang up your wife and told her to come home at once."

"I hope you're not trying to imply . . ."

"I'm not implying—anything! . . . Hullo! There's a car coming. I'll bet you what you like it's Madame Grandmaison. Would you be good enough not to tell her anything?"

A ring at the front door. Footsteps in the hall. Some whispered talk. Then the maid peeped in through the half-open door. Why did she say nothing? Why was she casting nervous glances at the master of the house?

"Well? What is it?" he asked impatiently.

"I thought I'd better . . ."

The Inspector pushed past her. In the hall was only a chauffeur in uniform. Maigret went straight to the point.

"So you lost Madame Grandmaison on the way here?" he asked.

"Well, sir, she . . . she . . ."

"Where did she get down?"

"At the Deauville turning. She was feeling ill."

In the study the mayor was already on his feet, breathing heavily, a stern look on his face.

"Wait for me!" he shouted to the chauffeur.

Maigret's bulky form blocked the way. He hesitated.

"I suppose you won't prevent me . . . ?"

"Certainly not. You're right. *We'll* go there right away!"

12. *The Unfinished Letter*

THE car halted at a cross-roads. Open country, no houses in sight. The chauffeur looked round for orders.

Since leaving Ouistreham a great change had come over the mayor. So far he had always kept his nerves under control, retained something of his dignity even in the most trying circumstances. All that was ended. He had lost self-control, given way to something uncommonly like panic. And his appearance, the scars and bruises on his face, emphasized his plight. All the way he had been gazing nervously out of the window.

When the car stopped he shot an inquiring glance at Maigret. But the Inspector indulged in the malicious pleasure of asking:

"Well, what's our next move?"

Not a soul on the road or in the orchards beside it. Obviously Madame Grandmaison had not alighted merely to feast her eyes on the landscape. If, on reaching this point, she had sent her chauffeur home, it was because she had an appointment, or had suddenly caught sight of some-one with whom she wished to have a private interview.

The air was laden with the fumes of rain-soaked earth; the leaves were dripping. Cows stared at the car, without ceasing to munch. . . .

The mayor seemed to expect to discover his wife hiding behind a hedge or tree-trunk, for he kept on peering anxiously in all directions.

"See that?" Maigret sounded as if he were helping out a novice.

There was no mistaking the tire-prints on the Dives road. A car had stopped there, had had some trouble in turning owing to the narrowness of the road, and gone off again.

"A light lorry. Pretty old," Maigret observed, and told the chauffeur to follow up the tracks.

They soon stopped again. Well before Dives the tracks petered out where a stony by-road led off to the right. Monsieur Grandmaison was still on the alert, a glint of anger mingling with the apprehension in his eyes.

"What do you make of it?"

"There's a village over there, five hundred yards down that road."

"In that case we'd better leave the car here."

Weariness gave Maigret an air of almost inhuman apathy. He moved like a sleep-walker, or a machine carried forward by its own momentum. Anyone seeing the two men walking down the road would have imagined that the mayor was in command, Maigret an underling.

They went past a cottage with fowls roaming around it; a woman on the doorstep eyed them wonderingly. Presently they came out at the back of the village church, which was hardly larger than the cottage. On their left was a tobacconist's.

Maigret displayed his empty pouch. "Wait a moment, please."

The shop dealt in groceries and household sundries as well as tobacco. An old man emerged from a room with a vaulted ceiling and called his daughter to serve the customer. Through the half-open door Maigret had a glimpse of a telephone fixed on the wall.

"How long is it since my friend came and used your 'phone?"

The girl answered promptly:

"Oh, quite an hour."

"Ah! Then the lady turned up all right?"

"Yes. As a matter of fact, she called in here to ask her way. It's quite easy to find. The last house in the lane on the right."

He went out, composed as ever. Monsieur Grandmaison was waiting in front of the church, casting agitated glances round him. If he goes on behaving like that, Maigret thought, we'll have all the village turning out to watch us!

"It's just struck me," he said in a low tone, "that we may as well divide forces for this job. Will you make searches on the left, where the fields begin? I'll do the same thing on the right."

A gleam of satisfaction, which he vainly tried to hide, showed in the mayor's eyes. Maigret saw what was in his mind. He hoped to be the first to find Madame Grandmaison, and have the opportunity for a private talk with her.

"Right you are!" he replied with feigned indifference.

The village consisted of some twenty houses. At one point they were huddled side by side and there was an apology for a road between them, littered with dung. It was still raining—a fine misty drizzle—and nobody was about. But curtains were drawn stealthily aside. Maigret had glimpses of old women, wizened peasant faces, peeping at the strangers.

On the outskirts, just beside a meadow in which two horses were scampering about, was a small low hut, with a curiously humped roof and two steps leading to the door. Maigret looked back, listened. He heard the mayor's footfalls at the other end of the village. Without knocking, he walked in.

The room was in darkness but for the glow of a wood

fire. As he entered there was a rustling in the shadows. He glimpsed a dark form, a blob of white—an old woman's cap.

She shuffled up to him, bent-backed.

"What do you want?" she asked.

The room was stuffy; there was a mingled stench of fowls, boiled cabbage, litter. Chickens were pecking round the logs beside the fire. Maigret's head almost touched the ceiling.

He noticed a door at the far end. He knew he must act quickly. Without a word he went up to the door, threw it open.

Madame Grandmaison was sitting at a table, writing; Martineau beside her.

There was a moment's pause. Madame Grandmaison jumped up from the rush-bottomed chair in which she was sitting. Martineau's first movement was to grab the sheet of paper and crush it in his hand. Instinctively the two drew closer together.

There were only two rooms in the hut. This one was the old woman's bedroom. On the whitewashed walls hung two portraits and some framed color-prints. A high four-poster bed. The table at which Madame Grandmaison had been writing was a wash-stand; the basin stood on the floor.

Maigret opened the conversation by saying:

"Your husband will be here in a few minutes."

"Your doing, I presume," said the man furiously.

"Hush, Raymond."

So she called him by his Christian name, and that name was not Jean but Raymond. . . . Maigret went to the door, listened, came back to them.

"Will you give me the letter you were writing?"

They gazed at each other. Madame Grandmaison was

pale, her features drawn and weary. Last time Maigret saw her she had been engaged in what the social set to which she belonged regarded as a woman's most exalted function—playing the part of hostess.

She had played it expertly, he had noticed; he had been struck by the conventional but charming amiability with which she dispensed cups of tea and smiles, or responded to a compliment.

He had pictured her life, with its daily round of visits, entertaining, supervising the children's education. Two or three months a year at fashionable resorts. A mild desire to fascinate. But less interest in her "appeal" than in the world's esteem.

No doubt something of all that remained in the woman standing before him. But there was something else. Actually she was displaying more self-possession, not to say courage, than the man beside her, who indeed looked like breaking down completely.

"Give him the letter," she said, noticing that he was about to tear it up. There were only two lines of it.

Dear Headmaster,
  Would you be so good as to . . .

It was in the characteristic handwriting—tall, with a backward slope—of girls educated in the early nineteen-hundreds in fashionable schools.

"You had two telephone calls this morning, hadn't you? One from your husband. Or, to be accurate, you rang him up to say you were coming to Ouistreham. Then Monsieur Martineau called you, and asked you to come here. He sent a delivery-van to meet you at the turning."

On the table, behind the inkpot, lay something that Maigret had not noticed at first: a wad of thousand-franc notes.

Martineau followed his gaze. Too late to do anything. A rush of hopelessness came over him. He sank on to the old woman's bed and stared forlornly at the floor.

"Was it you who brought him that money?"

What Maigret had come to regard as the characteristic atmosphere, so to speak, of this case, settled in again. He had been conscious of it in the mayor's study when he had found Louis belaboring the mayor and neither would vouchsafe a word of explanation. Then, again, in the schooner's cabin, where none of the three men would speak. A sort of passive resistance. A conspiracy of silence.

"As your son's at *Stanislas*, I presume this letter is intended for the headmaster of that school. As for the money . . . Why, of course! When the schooner ran aground, Martineau had to swim for it. He must have left his wallet on board. You brought him this money to pay . . ." He broke off, went on in a different tone: "The other men on board, Martineau—did they get ashore safely?"

The man hesitated; then, almost involuntarily, it seemed, gave a slight nod.

"I won't ask you where they're hiding. I know you wouldn't tell me."

"That's so."

"*What's* so?" The door had just been flung open. The mayor barked out the question. He had changed out of recognition. He was now in a towering rage, his fists clenched, breathing heavily. His eyes roved from his wife's face to Martineau; thence to the bundle of notes on the table. But behind the truculence of his gaze there lurked a secret fear, perhaps a premonition of disaster.

"What's he been saying? What new lie has he invented? And she, why should she—?" His voice broke. He paused for breath. Maigret held himself in readiness to intervene, if necessary. " 'That's so,' he said. What did he mean?

What's happening? What plot's being hatched here? That money—whose is it?"

The old woman could be heard in the next room shuffling towards the front door, calling her fowls.

"Chick! Chick! Chick!"

A patter of Indian corn on the steps. Indignant cackles from a neighbor's hen as she shooed it away. "'Tain't for you, Blackie. Get out of here!"

In the bedroom, silence. A portentous silence, brooding, mournful as the gray rain-blurred sky.

Fear lay behind it. All these people were hag-ridden: Martineau, the woman, the mayor. And each, it seemed, was haunted by a different fear—an unshared secret.

Deliberately Maigret took a solemn tone, like a judge's on the bench.

"My instructions are to discover and to arrest the murderer of Captain Joris, who was wounded by a shot from a revolver, and to whom, shortly after, a fatal dose of strychnine was administered in his house. Has any one of you a statement to make bearing on this crime?"

Till now, no one had noticed that the room was unheated. Suddenly everyone felt cold. Each syllable had rung out, as in a church. And certain words—"strychnine," "a fatal dose"—seemed still vibrating in the air.

Especially the final phrase: "Has any one of you a statement to make?"

Martineau was the first to drop his eyes. Madame Grandmaison gazed first at her husband, then at the Norwegian; her eyes glowed darkly.

But no one spoke. Nor did any of them face up to Maigret's searching gaze.

Two minutes passed. Three minutes. The old woman could be heard putting logs on her fire in the next room.

Again Maigret spoke. His tone was intentionally flat, unemotional.

"In the name of the Law, Jean Martineau, I arrest you."

A scream. Madame Grandmaison made a hasty movement towards Martineau, but, before she reached his side, sank to the floor, fainting.

The mayor deliberately turned his back on her and stared sullenly at the wall.

Martineau heaved a deep sigh, of weariness or resignation. He did not dare to go to the help of the woman lying on the floor.

It was left to Maigret to fetch the water-jug and do what he could for her. He opened the door, called to the old woman:

"Some vinegar, please."

Fumes of vinegar joined the curious medley of smells pervading the hut.

Several minutes passed before Madame Grandmaison came to. After some nervous sobs she relapsed into a state of almost complete prostration.

"Do you feel up to walking?"

She nodded, then rose to her feet. Somehow she managed to drag herself along.

"Follow me," Maigret commanded the two men. "I hope that *this time*, anyhow, I can count on your compliance with my orders."

Her eyes agape, the old woman watched them cross her kitchen. As they went out she called after them:

"You'll be back for lunch, won't you, Monsieur Raymond?"

"Raymond" again, Maigret noted. The man shook his head.

The four of them walked through the village. As they

passed the tobacconist's Martineau slowed down, hesitated, and turned to Maigret.

"Excuse me, but I can't be sure of coming here again and I don't want to leave debts behind me. I owe them for a glass of rum, a packet of cigarettes, and a telephone call."

Maigret paid. They walked round the church. The car was waiting at the end of the by-road. The Inspector told the others to get in; pondered a moment before speaking to the chauffeur.

"Ouistreham, please. Stop at the police station first."

Not a word passed during the journey. From the hueless sky the rain poured down, and the wind, which was rising again, tossed the dripping branches of the trees.

At the police station Maigret asked Martineau to alight and gave instructions to the sergeant.

"Keep him in the lock-up. You're responsible for him. . . . Any news?"

"The tug's come. They're waiting for the tide."

The car moved on. As they were passing the harbor Maigret called another halt, and stepped out.

It was noon. The lock-keepers were at their posts; a steamer was due in from Caen. The strip of sand along the foreshore had dwindled and white spray was breaking almost on the dunes.

On the right a crowd had gathered to watch an exciting scene. The Trouville tug was anchored less than five hundred yards from the shore. A small boat was struggling through the waves to the *Saint Michel*, which had almost righted herself with the rising tide.

Maigret noticed that the mayor, too, was watching the scene from behind the windows of the car. Captain Delcourt came out of the café. Maigret went up to him.

"Will they manage it?"

"They ought to. I've had men on board her for the last

two hours, throwing out ballast. The only danger's if the tow-ropes break." He looked up, searching the sky, like a man reading a map, for forecasts of a change in the wind. "Only we've got to get it done before the tide turns."

Catching sight of the mayor and his wife in the car, he greeted them deferentially, but his eyes strayed back to Maigret.

"Any fresh developments?"

"Can't say."

Lucas, however, had news to give. But before doing so he drew his chief aside.

"We've got Louis."

"Really?"

"Yes, and it was his own fault. This morning the Dives police spotted some foot-prints in the fields—the foot-prints of a man who'd walked straight ahead, scrambling over fences. The tracks led to the Orne, to a place where a fisherman keeps his boat pulled up on the bank. Well, the boat was on the other side of the river."

"In other words, they'd crossed it?"

"Yes. They landed on the beach, nearly opposite the *Saint Michel*. Just there, at the edge of the dunes—"

"There's a little ruined chapel."

"Ah, so you know it?"

"The Chapel of Our Lady of the Dunes."

"Exactly. That's where they rounded him up. He was crouching in the chapel, watching the salvage party at work. When I came he was begging the police not to take him away at once. He wanted to stay till the schooner was afloat again. I agreed to that. He's there now, in hand-cuffs. He's in terror they'll lose his ship, and he's bawling orders to the tug. Like to go and have a look at him?"

"Maybe. But not just now."

He remembered that he had the other two, Grandmaison and his wife, waiting in the car.

"Think we'll get to the bottom of it?" As Maigret did not answer, Lucas went on: "Personally, I'm getting to think we never shall. They're lying, every man-jack of 'em. And the ones that don't tell lies won't speak, though I'm certain they're in the know! It really looks as if everyone in Ouistreham has had a hand in Joris's death!"

But the Inspector merely shrugged his shoulders and walked away, grunting:

"See you presently."

Back at the car, he said to the chauffeur, much to the latter's surprise:

"Home, please."

It sounded as if he were referring to his own home, addressing someone in his service.

"Do you mean the house at Caen, sir?"

As a matter of fact he hadn't meant it; but an idea had just occurred to him.

"Yes."

Monsieur Grandmaison scowled. His wife appeared to have lost the power of reacting. She seemed content to let thinks take their course, to follow the line of least resistance.

Between the city gate and the Rue du Four at least fifty hats were raised as the car passed by. Everyone seemed to know Monsieur Grandmaison's Renault. And the salutations were obsequious. The shipowner might have been a feudal lord visiting his domain.

"Merely a matter of routine," said Maigret in an easy tone as the car pulled up. "You must excuse me for bringing you here. But, as I think I told you, I intend to have the inquiry finished by this evening."

It was a quiet street, flanked by stately private residences such as are to be found nowadays only in provincial towns. A courtyard preceded the house, which was built in solid, age-grimed stone. On the gateway was a brass plate: *Anglo-Norman Navigation Company*.

In the courtyard a notice-board with an arrow, inscribed: *Office*. Another inscribed: *Counting-house*. A third: *Office Hours*, 9 A.M. *to* 4 P.M.

The journey from Ouistreham had taken only ten minutes. It was a little after noon. Most of the employees were away at their lunch, but a few were still on duty in the dark majestic-looking offices furnished in mid-nineteenth-century style and sumptuously carpeted.

"I suggest, madame, that you go up to your rooms for the present. Later on, perhaps, I may ask for the favor of a few minutes' talk with you."

The ground floor consisted exclusively of offices. The entrance-hall was spacious, flanked by wrought-iron candelabra. A marble staircase led up to the first floor, which was the Grandmaisons' residence.

The mayor waited sulkily for Maigret to give him instructions what to do. He had turned up his overcoat collar and drawn down his hat to conceal from his staff the condition of his face after the previous night's rough handling.

"Well, what do you want of me?" he asked.

"Nothing very much. Only to authorize me to roam about this place as I think fit—to get the hang of it, so to speak."

"Want me with you?"

"Not in the least."

"In that case, if you've no objection, I'll go upstairs and see how my wife is feeling."

The tone in which he spoke of her now was in marked contrast with his behavior in the old woman's cottage.

Maigret watched him go up the stairs, then went to the far end of the hall and made sure there was only one exit from the building.

He next went out into the street, hunted up a police officer and posted him at the gate.

"Got it? Let everyone leave who wants to, except Monsieur Grandmaison. Do you know him by sight?"

"Course I do. But—but what's he been up to? A gentleman like him! Why, he's President of the Chamber of Commerce!"

"That's fine!"

A door opened off the hall, on the right: *Office*. After knocking, Maigret opened it and walked in. An odor of cigar-smoke hung in the air, but no one was to be seen.

On the left, another door: *Board Room*. Here, too, reigned an atmosphere of studied dignity. An elaborately decorated ceiling, a deep-pile dark red carpet, lavishly gilt wall-paper. One felt that in such a room no one would dare to raise his voice. One pictured dignified, frock-coated gentlemen, puffing fat cigars, seated round the table in solemn conclave.

A well-established, solid House: the typical provincial concern, handed down from father to son, generation after generation.

"Monsieur Grandmaison? His signature's as good as gold!"

Maigret entered the great man's private office. It had been furnished in the Empire style, doubtless as more becoming for a merchant prince. On the wall hung pictures of ships, statistical charts, multicolored graphs.

As he was pacing up and down the room, his hands thrust in his pockets, a door opened and a startled face peeped in. An old, white-haired man's.

"Please, who . . . ?"

"I'm a police officer," Maigret cut in. Was it fondness for theatrical effects that made him rap out the words so peremptorily?

The old fellow looked horror-struck, and began to tremble.

"Come, come! There's nothing to be alarmed about. Your employer's asked me to hold an inquiry. You, I presume, are—"

"The Chief Cashier," the old man hastened to explain.

"Ah, yes. You're the man who's been in the firm for . . . for . . ."

"Forty-two years. Since Monsieur Charles's time."

"Quite so. And that's your office, through that side-door, isn't it? Really, from what I hear, it's you who run the business—in a manner of speaking. Isn't that so?"

Maigret was on velvet. A glimpse of the premises, then of this old employee, had been enough to give him his cue.

"That's only natural, isn't it, sir? When Monsieur Ernest's away . . ."

"Monsieur Ernest?"

"Yes. Monsieur Grandmaison, I mean. I've known him since he was a boy, that's why I always call him 'Monsieur Ernest.'"

With seeming casualness Maigret had been moving, as they spoke, towards the old man's office. A humble sanctum, to which, presumably, the public were not admitted. The scantiness of the furniture was made up for by a copious array of files and ledgers.

A packet of sandwiches lay on the cluttered-up table. A small coffee-pot steamed on the stove.

"I see you have your meals here, Monsieur . . . ?"

"Bernardin. But everyone calls me 'Old Bernard.' I live all alone, so there's no point going home to lunch. . . . Of course! It's about the theft we had last week that

Monsieur Ernest's called you in. He should have told me. It's all been fixed up. A youngster took two thousand francs from the cash. His uncle's made it good, and the young chap's promised to turn over a new leaf. He's only a boy, sir. He'd got into bad company. . . . You understand, sir, don't you?"

"Quite. We'll go into that later. But don't mind me. Carry on with your lunch, please. . . . It comes to this, then. You were Monsieur Charles's right-hand man before Monsieur Ernest took over."

"I was cashier. There wasn't a Chief Cashier in those days. In fact, the post was created for my benefit," he added proudly.

"Is Monsieur Ernest Monsieur Charles's only son?"

"Yes. There was a daughter who married a business man, but she died in childbirth, as did the child."

"What about Monsieur Raymond?"

The old man looked up quickly.

"Ah! Has Monsieur Ernest told you about him?" he asked in a more guarded tone.

"Was he one of the family?"

"A cousin. A Grandmaison too. Only he was a poor one. His father'd died abroad. . . . It's like that in all families, isn't it, sir?"

"Why, of course!" Maigret repressed a smile.

"Monsieur Ernest's father had more or less adopted him. I mean, he'd given him a post in the firm."

No good beating about the bush. All this had got to be straightened out.

"Just a moment, Monsieur Bernard. Let's get it quite clear. The founder of the Anglo-Norman was Monsieur Charles Grandmaison, I understand. Monsieur Charles Grandmaison had an only son, Monsieur Ernest, who is now running the business. Is that correct?"

"Yes." The old man was beginning to take fright. He couldn't understand why he was being subjected to this cross-examination.

"Right. Monsieur Charles had a brother who died abroad. He, too, left an only son, Monsieur Raymond Grandmaison."

"Yes. But I don't . . ."

"Let me continue, please. . . . Go ahead with your lunch. . . . Monsieur Raymond Grandmaison, who was an orphan and penniless, was 'more or less adopted' by his uncle. What was the post that he was given?"

The old man seemed a little embarrassed.

"Well, he was put into the freight department. As a sort of sub-manager."

"Quite so. Then Monsieur Charles Grandmaison died. Monsieur Ernest took over. Monsieur Raymond kept his job on. That right?"

"Yes."

"One day there was a quarrel. Wait a bit! Was Monsieur Ernest already married when the quarrel took place?"

"I don't know if I should . . ."

"Let me tell you this. If you don't want to get into trouble with the law of the land—and that wouldn't be a nice thing for a man of your age—I advise you to speak out."

"Trouble with the law? I don't follow. Has Monsieur Raymond come back?"

"That's neither here nor there. I asked: Was Monsieur Ernest married then?"

"No. He got married after that."

"Right. Monsieur Ernest was head of the firm; his cousin, Raymond, a sub-manager. What was the trouble about?"

"I don't feel authorized . . ."

"*I* authorize you. Go on."

"It's like that in all families. Monsieur Ernest was like his father, a very steady man. Even at the age when most young fellows kick over the traces he was like that."

"And Monsieur Raymond?"

"Just the opposite."

"Well . . . ?"

"I'm the only one here, besides Monsieur Ernest, who knows about it. We found the accounts had been tampered with. Large sums were involved."

"And then?"

"Monsieur Raymond vanished. I mean, instead of prosecuting him, Monsieur Ernest told him to go abroad."

"To Norway?"

"That I can't say. I never heard tell of him again."

"And, soon after, Monsieur Ernest got married?"

"That's right; some months later."

Letter-filing cabinets, painted a dingy green, lined the walls of the gloomy little room. The old employee did not seem to be relishing his meal; he was worried and, above all, furious with himself for so tamely submitting to being "pumped."

"How long ago was that?"

"Let me think. . . . The year when the canal was widened. Just under fifteen years ago."

For some minutes they had been hearing someone moving to and fro in the room above.

"The dining-room?" Maigret asked.

"Yes."

Suddenly there was a rush of hurried footsteps, followed by a dull thud, the sound of a body falling on the floor.

Old Bernard went whiter than the paper that had wrapped his sandwiches.

13. *The House Opposite*

MONSIEUR GRANDMAISON was dead. Stretched full-length on the carpet, his head beside a table-leg, his feet against the window-jamb, he looked enormous. He had bled very little. The bullet had passed between two ribs and pierced the heart.

The revolver had slipped from his hand as it relaxed, and lay an inch or so away.

Madame Grandmaison was not weeping. Leaning against the mantelpiece, she was staring down at her husband with a look of profound bewilderment.

"It's all over," Maigret said quietly as he rose to his feet.

A dismal room, austerely furnished. Dark curtains. The cheerless light of a gray day.

"Did he say anything to you?"

She shook her head. Then, with an effort, managed to bring out some words of explanation.

"Ever since we got home he'd been pacing up and down the room. Once or twice he turned to me and I thought he was going to say something. Quite suddenly he fired—I hadn't even noticed he was holding a revolver."

She spoke as women do under the stress of emotion—as though she had difficulty in following the thread of her ideas. But her eyes remained tearless.

Obviously she had never loved Grandmaison; anyhow, never loved him passionately. He was her husband. She had done her duty by him. And years of life in common had slowly formed a bond of mild affection. No more.

Gazing at her husband's body, she showed none of those signs of desperate grief which, when a loved one dies, cannot be repressed. Wearily, but with steady eyes, she turned to Maigret.

"Was it he?"

"Yes. It was."

Silence. The bleak light from the window fell full on the huge form stretched on the carpet. Watching the woman, the Inspector saw her gaze shift towards the street, settle on something just across it. Her eyes grew dim with a vague regret.

"May I ask you two or three questions before anyone comes?"

She nodded.

"You knew Raymond before you met your husband, didn't you?"

"I lived in the house across the road."

A gray house, rather like her present home. Over the entrance a notary's brass sign.

"I loved Raymond. He was in love with me. His cousin, too, was in love with me—after his manner."

"And the two were very different, weren't they?"

"You have seen something of Ernest lately. Well, he was just the same then. Cold, with nothing young about him. Raymond had a bad reputation. He led a dissipated life, by small-town standards. Because of that, and because he had no money, my father disapproved of my marrying him."

Her voice was low, strangely composed under the tragic circumstances. . . . The summing-up of a frustrated life.

"Were you . . . Raymond's mistress?"

Her eyelashes fluttered. She did not shake her head.

"Then he went away, didn't he?"

"Yes, without letting anyone know. At night. I only

heard of it through his cousin. And took with him some of the firm's money."

"Then Ernest married you. Am I right in supposing he's not the father of your son?"

"Yes. Raymond is the father of my boy. When he went away and left me I knew I was going to have a baby. There was nobody I could turn to. Ernest kept asking me to marry him. You understand, don't you? In a small town like this everybody knows everybody, our two houses faced each other, only the street between, and—"

"Did you tell Ernest the truth?"

"Yes. He knew it when he married me. My baby was born in Italy. I stayed there for a year, to prevent gossip. I thought my husband's attitude was something rather fine, romantic."

"And now?"

She turned away; her eyes had just fallen on the dead body.

"Ah," she sighed, "I'm not so sure now. I think he loved me, but in his own way. He'd always wanted me. Well, he got me. Do you see what I mean? It wasn't a generous impulse, as I'd thought. After our marriage he lived exactly as before—for himself only. I was just part of his establishment: a sort of superior housekeeper, the lady of the house. I don't know if he had any news of Raymond after that. I remember one day my son asking who it was when he happened to see Raymond's photo in an old album. My husband merely said, 'Oh, that's a cousin of mine, who's gone to the bad!'"

Maigret was in a brown study. His imagination had been stirred; pictures were forming in his mind of this woman's life. Not of hers alone: of the "inside story" of a firm, a family. Fifteen years it had lasted. New steamers had been acquired. This room had been the frequent scene of social functions: tea-parties, bridge-parties; christening parties too!

Summer holidays at Ouistreham or a mountain resort. . . .

Madame Grandmaison was exhausted. She sank into a chair; passed a limp hand over her forehead.

"I can't make it out," she murmured weakly. "That captain—he was a complete stranger to me. Do you really think . . . ?"

Maigret pricked up his ears, then opened the door. The old cashier was standing outside, too timid to knock. As he gazed at the Inspector a question hovered on his lips.

"Monsieur Grandmaison's dead. Please call the family doctor. Don't let any of the servants or employees know of this, for the present."

He shut the door, all but took his pipe from his pocket, shrugged his shoulders.

He was conscious of an unexpected feeling of respect and understanding for this woman whom, the first time he had seen her, he had dismissed as a mere society butterfly.

"Was it your husband who told you to go to Paris yesterday?"

"Yes. I'd no idea Raymond was in France. My husband asked me to call at my son's school and take him with me for a few days' holiday on the south coast. It struck me as rather queer, but I did as he told me. When I reached the hotel, he rang me up and told me to come back without going to the school."

"Raymond telephoned when you were here this morning, didn't he?"

"Yes. He seemed dreadfully upset. He implored me to bring some money. He said our future—the future of all of us—was at stake."

"Didn't he say anything incriminating your husband?"

"No. And when we were in the cottage he didn't even mention him. He only told me that some sailors, friends of his, had to leave the country and needed money. He said something about a shipwreck."

The doctor, an old family friend, came in. He gazed at the dead body with consternation.

"Monsieur Grandmaison has killed himself." Maigret's tone was heavily official. "It's for you to decide what form of illness led to his sudden death. That's your business. As for the police end—I'll see to it."

He went up to Madame Grandmaison to take leave of her.

"You haven't told me why . . ." she began.

"Raymond will tell you all one day. One last question. On September the sixteenth your son was at Ouistreham with your husband, wasn't he?"

"Yes. He stayed there till the twentieth."

Maigret bowed himself out, tramped heavily down the stairs, trudged through the office, his shoulders sagging, a feeling of oppression on his chest. Once in the street, he breathed more freely. For some minutes he stood bareheaded in the rain, and its contact seemed to brace him up, dispel the morbid atmosphere of the house.

A last look at the windows. Another at those of the house opposite, the scene of Madame Grandmaison's girlhood.

The Inspector sighed. . . .

"Come!"

He had opened the door of the cell in which Raymond was confined. Beckoning, he led the way into the street; then started down the road leading to the harbor.

Raymond seemed puzzled, and a shade perturbed, by this abrupt release.

"Still nothing to tell me?" Maigret inquired with seeming gruffness.

"Nothing."

"So you'll take your sentence lying down, eh?"

"I shall tell the judge I'm innocent of murder."

"But you'll not tell him the truth?"

Raymond lowered his eyes. The sea was coming into sight. The tug could be heard whistling as it steamed towards the jetty with the *Saint Michel* in tow.

In a carefully matter-of-fact tone Maigret said:

"Grandmaison's dead."

"What? What's that you said?" Raymond clutched his arm and squeezed it excitedly. "He's . . . ?"

"He committed suicide an hour ago, in his house."

"Did he . . . did he say anything?"

"No. He paced up and down his dining-room for a quarter of an hour. Then he shot himself. That's all."

In the distance, beside the lock, a crowd had gathered to watch the salvage operations.

"So now, Raymond Grandmaison, you can tell me the truth. As a matter of fact, I've a pretty shrewd idea of it already. You were trying to get back your son, weren't you?"

No answer.

"You enlisted helpers. One of them was Captain Joris. And, as ill luck would have it . . ."

"Stop! If you only knew!"

"Let's keep clear of the crowd. Come this way."

They took a path leading down to the empty beach, on which great waves were breaking.

"Did you really abscond with some of the firm's money?"

"Ah, so Hélène told you. . . ." There was a vicious edge to his voice. "And of course Ernest gave her his own version of the miserable story. I don't claim to have been a plaster saint—far from it! I was out for a good time. And, for a while, I had a mania for gambling. The usual ups and downs. One day, I don't deny it, I helped myself to some of the firm's money. My cousin found it out.

"I promised to pay it back by installments. I begged him not to ruin my good name.

"He agreed, but only on one condition; for he was quite prepared to report the matter to the police.

"The condition was that I should go abroad. And never set foot again in France."

A wry smile twisted his lips. He was silent for some moments before continuing.

"Most fellows in my place would have gone South, or East. I had a fancy for the North. I made my home in Norway. No letters came to me from France. The letters I wrote Hélène were unanswered. I learnt only yesterday that she never received them.

"I wrote to my cousin. He, too, never replied. I don't want to make myself out better than I am, and I won't try to play on your feelings by talking about frustrated love and all the rest of it. No, at first I really didn't think much about Hélène. (You can't complain I'm not being frank with you!) I worked, and it was one damned setback after another! It was only at night that I sometimes gave way to a sort of vague regret.

"Yes, I really had rough luck! A business I started went phut. For years it was touch and go—and don't forget I was a stranger in a strange land.

"I'd changed my name. I changed my nationality too; it was easier for me to do business as a Norwegian.

"Now and again I ran across officers serving on French ships; that's how I learnt, one day, I had a son. Only—I couldn't feel quite sure. I worked out the dates. . . . It grew to an obsession. I even wrote to Ernest. Begged him to tell me the truth, to let me return to France, if only for a day or two. He wired: '*Arrest immediate on crossing frontier.*'

"Years passed. I worked like a slave—money-making. A dog's life. And all the time I felt a sort of emptiness. Something had snapped inside me.

"At Tromsö it's pitch-dark for three months in the year. The darkness preys on one's nerves. There were moments when I was half mad with rage.

"I set myself a task: to become as rich as my cousin. It was a sort of dope, I suppose. . . . But I brought it off, thanks to the cod-roe industry. And it was when I'd brought it off that my anger really boiled up.

"I decided to *act* at last. After fifteen years! I returned to France. I hung about this town. One day I saw my son on the beach. And had a glimpse of Hélène.

"I couldn't understand. No, I couldn't understand how I'd lived all those years without my son. . . . Do you see what I mean, I wonder?

"I bought a boat. It had to be done in a clandestine way, as my cousin would have had me arrested without the least compunction. He'd preserved the evidence against me.

"You've seen my men. Good chaps, though their appearance is against them, I'll admit. We fixed it all up.

"That night Ernest Grandmaison had my boy staying with him. No one else was in the house. To make things even surer, I'd roped in Captain Joris. I'd met him in Norway when he was in the merchant service.

"He was an acquaintance of the mayor's. I asked him to call on the mayor, on some pretext or other, and hold him in conversation while Louis and I kidnapped my son.

"Poor Joris! I little guessed I was leading him to his death. While he was talking to my cousin in the study we got in by the back door. As we were creeping along the passage one of us knocked over a broom.

"Grandmaison heard the noise. He thought he was being burgled and took his revolver from a drawer of his desk. What happened then? I haven't a notion. The passage was in darkness. There was a general mix-up.

"Joris must have followed Grandmaison from the study. A shot was fired.

"As ill luck would have it, it hit Joris in the head.

"I was half crazy. I had only one idea. For Hélène's sake nothing must leak out. There was no question of my going to the police and explaining things.

"Louis and I carried the wounded man to the *Saint Michel*. The first thing was to get in touch with a doctor. We sailed for England, did the crossing in a few hours.

"But then we couldn't land. No passports. Policemen on the quay. I'd studied medicine a bit in my youth. I did what I could for Joris, but it was a doctor's job. We crossed to Holland. There he was operated on. But the hospital refused to keep him unless we notified the authorities.

"The voyage north was a nightmare. Try to imagine what it meant—cooped up on board with Joris at the point of death.

"He needed a good month's rest and proper attention. I thought of taking him to Norway on the *Saint Michel*. But we happened to come across another schooner bound for the Lofoten Islands. I took passages in her for myself and Joris. We were safer at sea than on land.

"He stayed a week at my house. But there, too, people started talking, wondering who my mysterious guest could be.

"So off we went again. To Copenhagen. To Hamburg.

"Joris was recovering. The wound had healed. But he

had lost his reason and the power of speech. Put yourself in my place. What was I to do about him? Surely he stood a better chance of getting back to sanity in his home surroundings—that's how I saw it.

"Anyhow, I could make sure of his material welfare. I transferred three hundred thousand francs to his account, using his name.

"The next thing was to get him back to France. It was too risky for me to come with him to Ouistreham. But if I cast him adrift in Paris the police were bound to take charge of him sooner or later. Then he'd be identified and brought back home.

"And that's what happened. But there was one thing I couldn't possibly foresee. That my cousin, fearing that one day Joris might come out with the truth, would so brutally make away with him.

"For it's he who put the strychnine in the tumbler. All he had to do was to slip into the house by the back door on his way to his shooting-pit."

"And you," Maigret remarked slowly, "stuck to your scheme."

"I couldn't bring myself to give it up. I *needed* my son so badly. Only now my cousin was on his guard. The boy had been sent back to school, and I could see no way of getting at him there."

Most of the facts were known to Maigret. But, as he gazed at the scene before his eyes, now so familiar, and all fell into place, he could see more clearly into the bitter conflict that had been going on, unknown to all, between these two determined men. And the conflict had not been only between themselves. It had been with him too.

For, at all costs, the police had to be kept out of it. Neither could tell the truth.

"I came back on the *Saint Michel*."

"I know. And you dispatched Louis to the mayor. . . ."

The ghost of a smile hovered on Raymond's lips while the Inspector went on:

"That suited Louis's book—a chance of getting his own back on authority. He could go at it all out; his victim wouldn't dare to breathe a word. A glorious 'rough house'! He bullied Grandmaison into giving him a letter authorizing you to take the boy from the school."

"Yes. I was behind the house, with your man at my heels. Louis put the letter in the place we'd agreed on, and I shook off your sleuth! I scrounged a bicycle. At Caen I bought a car. There was no time to lose. While I went to fetch my son, Louis stayed with the mayor to see he didn't countermand his instructions to the school authorities. A useless precaution, as it turned out; he'd already sent Hélène to take the boy away before I got there.

"Then you had me arrested.

"I knew the game was up! Impossible to carry on while you were moving heaven and earth to get at the truth. My only chance was somehow to make my escape. You were bound to find out everything if we stayed.

"That explains last night's events. Bad luck still dogged us. The schooner ran aground. It was all we could do to swim ashore, and, as the last straw, I found I'd lost my wallet when I landed.

"No money. The police on my tracks. There was nothing for it but to ring up Hélène and ask her for a few thousand francs, enough to see the four of us across the frontier.

"Hélène came at once. But so did you! At every turn we were up against you. You dogged our steps, but we couldn't tell you the truth; I daren't warn you that you might well bring on another tragedy."

He stopped short. A worried look came into his eyes, and he asked in an uncertain voice:

"I say, *it is true* my cousin's dead?"

It had obviously struck him that Maigret might have laid a trap for him.

"It's true. He killed himself when he realized the truth was coming out. He knew it when I arrested you. He guessed that I'd done this only to give him time to think things over."

They had reached the jetty. The *Saint Michel* was gliding slowly past. An old fisherman lorded it at her helm.

A man rushed up, thrusting the watchers on the quay aside, and took a flying leap on to the schooner's deck.

It was Louis.

He had snapped the links between his handcuffs, given the men in charge of him the slip. Bundling the old fisherman to one side, he grasped the tiller.

"Ease down a bit, for God's sake!" he yelled to the men on board the tug. "You'll tear my bows out!"

"What's happened to the other two?" Maigret asked the man beside him.

"You were within a yard or two of them this morning. They were hiding in old Marie's woodshed!"

Lucas pushed his way through the crowd. He gave a start at seeing Raymond with the Inspector.

"Good news! We've got 'em!"

"Got whom?"

"Lannec and Célestin."

"Where are they?"

"The Dives police have just brought them here."

"Have them released at once. And tell them to come along to the harbor."

They could see, facing them, Joris's cottage. The previous night's storm had stripped the petals of the last roses in the garden. A face at the window: Julie wondering if it could really be her brother she saw at the schooner's helm.

The habitués of the *Sailors' Rest* were standing in a group near Captain Delcourt.

"The trouble I've had," sighed Maigret, "with those fellows and their damned evasive answers!"

Raymond smiled. "They're seamen."

"Exactly! And seamen can't stick a landlubber like myself prying into their affairs." He filled his pipe, ramming the tobacco home with little taps of his forefinger. After he had lit it he sighed again, and his brows wrinkled. "What the devil are we going to tell 'em?"

Ernest Grandmaison was dead. Was one bound to reveal the fact that he was a murderer?

"I suggest . . ." Raymond began.

"I wonder now . . . ? We might say that the crime was the work of some foreign sailor with a grudge against the Captain. And that he's gone back to his country. I'll think it over."

The crew of the tug were adjourning to the *Sailors' Rest*. They beckoned to the lock-keepers to join them.

Louis was roaming up and down his ship, running his hands over the woodwork, like the owner of a dog that's been lost and just come home, making sure it isn't injured anywhere.

"Ahoy, you!" Maigret shouted.

Louis gave a start, hesitated. The idea of coming to Maigret—or, rather, leaving his ship again—didn't appeal to him. Then he noticed Raymond, and looked as much surprised as Lucas had been.

"What the—"

"When can the *Saint Michel* go to sea again?"

"Right away, if she has to. Not a leak nowhere. Aye, she's a great little ship is the old *Saint Michel!*"

His gaze shifted to Raymond, who said:

"In that case, I'll ask you to have a cruise around, with Lannec and Célestin."

"What? Are they here?"

"They're coming. . . . Whoop it up, or whatever you fellows call it, for a week or two. But nowhere near Ouistreham. Give the people here time to forget about the *Saint Michel*."

"Might take my sister with us, to do the cooking. . . . She's a well-plucked 'un, is Julie."

Still, he wasn't too pleased with himself, because of Maigret. That business of the night before—dare he treat it as a joke?

"Hope you didn't find it too cold, sir, on the wharf?" he grinned.

He was standing near the edge of the quay. With a deft nudge of his elbow Maigret sent him spinning into the water.

"I can make the six o'clock train," the Inspector murmured. But he seemed to be in no hurry to move. He had taken a fancy to the little harbor, and was gazing at it almost sentimentally.

After all, didn't he know every nook and corner of it; hadn't he seen it under many aspects—shivering in the gray dawn, storm-swept, drenched in rain and sea-fog?

He turned to Raymond, who was dogging his steps.

"Going to Caen?"

"Not immediately. It would be unwise, I think. Better leave . . ."

"Leave time to do its work? Yes."

A quarter of an hour later, Lucas came back and asked where Maigret was. Someone pointed to the *Sailors' Rest*, in which the lamps had just been lit.

Through the misted panes he made out the Inspector's

burly form straddling a cane-seated chair. Puffing at his pipe, reaching now and then to the mug of beer beside him, he was listening to the sailors' yarns being swopped around him by men in sea-boots and sou'westers.

Good fellows all! And in the night train back to Paris Maigret heaved a sigh.

"Those three rascals must be feeling nice and cozy now in that cubby-hole of theirs." *Lucas' query.*

"What cubby-hole?"

"The cabin on the *Saint Michel*. Sitting round the swing-lamp, with the big glasses and a bottle of Hollands on that battered old table. And the stove roaring like billy-ho! . . . Give us a light, old chap."

ASW

31 May, 2018

speaking to Lucas!